Rhoda Broughton

Joan

A Tale: Vol. I.

Rhoda Broughton

Joan
A Tale: Vol. I.

ISBN/EAN: 9783337079123

Printed in Europe, USA, Canada, Australia, Japan

Cover: Foto ©Andreas Hilbeck / pixelio.de

More available books at **www.hansebooks.com**

JOAN

A Tale

BY

RHODA BROUGHTON

AUTHOR OF

"COMETH UP AS A FLOWER" "RED AS A ROSE IS SHE" "GOOD-BYE SWEET-
HEART!" "NANCY" "NOT WISELY BUT TOO WELL"

IN THREE VOLUMES

VOL. I.

LONDON

RICHARD BENTLEY AND SON

Publishers in Ordinary to Her Majesty the Queen

1876

JOAN.

PART I.

CHAPTER I.

"And ye shall walk in silk attire,
And siller hae to spare!"

OLFERSTAN is humming this
very softly to himself, half under
his breath, half over. A girl at
the house he is staying at sang it last night,
and it runs in his head yet; a girl whose
music leaves he turned, whose music stool
he screwed up, and three of whose fingers he
succeeded in squeezing when he gave her her

candle at bed-time. Wolferstan has not got
it on his conscience that he ever in all his life
missed an opportunity of squeezing a woman's
hand.

" And siller hae to spare !"

" Ah ! that is just what I am afraid she
will not have, poor soul !"

It is not the girl whose fingers he squeezed
of whom he is thinking, but another. It is
Easter Day, in the afternoon. Wolferstan
is sitting on an old tree trunk that once was
a stout oak-tree, but through whose dry old
veins not even this strong young spring,
vigorously awakening, can send the green
sap-blood racing. Before Wolferstan's eyes
spread the ups and downs, the dead fern and
live deer; the mighty single trees roomily
stretching great arms on all sides of them
into the free and wholesome air, and the
bosky coppices of an English park. In his
ears is the austere music of church bells from
different parishes, all seeming to tell with

solemn mirth that "Christ is risen." Wolferstan is not going to church. He went this
morning, and found her places in the hymn-
book (out of which he afterwards warbled
with her) for the girl with the fingers. He
is bound on a much disagreeabler errand now ;
and so he thinks. He is going to pay a visit
of condolence ; yes—to condole with a young
lady upon the loss of her grandfather.

The death of a grandfather is generally a
very supportable affliction. But a small
bottle would hold the tears that most people
shed for their grandparents. Most of us can
kiss that rod. But in the present case grandfather is a wide word. It means father,
mother, brother, sister, home, standing, soft
lying, high feeding, pretty nearly everything
that makes life a morsel to be eaten with
slow relish instead of a physic draught to be
quickly swallowed with wry faces. It is
difficult to offer comfort to a person who has
lost all these at one sweep. So Wolferstan
feels. Though he has been sitting on his

tree trunk for a good half-hour, cudgelling such brains as God has given him, nothing that sounds even to himself in the least degree consolatory occurs to him. The only thing that will persistently recur to him— often and angrily as he has driven it away as utterly inadmissible — is the old and homely saw that " it is no use crying over spilt milk." He cannot get rid of it. It comes back like a gnat, and sticks like a burr. Its rude philosophy thrusts itself between him and all suitabler forms of speech.

In despair he jumps up at last, and begins to walk through the quickening freshening grass towards the great old Hall, with four cold gray towers ivy-muffled, that stands amid level velvet gardens fronting him. The bells are still ringing. The air is temperately cool; neither balmy nor yet sharp : the sky looks high and chill and palely coloured. Heaven seems far off, though it is Easter Day. Last time that he was here it was winter, and the hounds met here. A small bright rime lay on the grass; flashes of scarlet warmed up the cold and sunless colours of the weather-scarred gray walls. The old Squire was pottering about on his old horse. Well, the old Squire is dead now! dead suddenly. He was not among those who fumble and bungle long at the lock which shuts in the great secret. I think that more people than used to do so, go suddenly nowadays. We have increased the speed of our travelling over this earth, why not also the quickness of our journey from this world into the next? Anyhow, he went quickly: not even in his own house or his own bed; but in a public place, at a public meeting. With one stoop forward of his gray head—with one groaning breath, he went and took the great and unavoidable stride without time for any pain or fear.

Poor old Squire! Yes, and that same day on which the hounds met here, Joan stood on the top of the steps in a mouse-coloured velvet gown, shading with one hand the laughter of her eyes from the low cool winter sun which stared so hard at her. And the sun had good taste : she was worth staring at. He has reached the Hall door by now; mounted the steps, and rung the bell.

"Nothing is changed!" he says to himself with a sort of irrational surprise, looking back at the park across which he has come, and at a herd of stags that are trooping from one glade to another, with a tossing of great horns and whisking of tiny tails.

But after all why should the grass look withered and the deer's plump flanks fall in because an old man is, dead? It would be much odder if they did. At least the footman who opens the door is changed. He has moulted his gay blue and yellow plumage, and now the sable rook is not blacker than he.

As Wolferstan follows him through half a dozen rooms, big and little, he looks round him affectionately. One always feels rather

fondly towards a house where one has been
happy, and Wolferstan has had many jovial
moments in this one. Here stand the statues
—just as they did on the night of the theatricals—when Joan made such a sweet widow
that he very nearly asked her to run the
chance of being his. Here is Psyche,
slenderly nude, with her butterfly on her
finger. The little serpent is still stinging
Eurydice's cold white heel, and Hadrian still
stands stern in his panoply.

When at last they reach the sitting-room,
towards which they finally tend, they find it
empty. In it there is neither man nor mouse,
nor woman either. The only live thing is a
small faint fire that the sun is trying hard to
kill—a little fire from whose dull heart a red
glow shines reflected in the old Dutch tiles,
where Eve's gluttony and Noah's carouse are
devoutly, yet grotesquely, wrought in blue
and white. Near the hearth is drawn up an
arm-chair, which, though it is not at all rucked
up or disarranged, as it infallibly would have

been had a man occupied it, yet has the indescribable air of having been lately sat in. A book with its back still warm and warped from having been held over the fire gapes half open on the table. There are flowers— flowers everywhere! They seem to have walked in through the open door of the neighbouring conservatory.

She has not come yet: perhaps she does not mean to come at all. He walks about nervously, saying over to himself his prepared speech, and trying to keep the spilt milk out of it. He strolls into the conservatory, and looks at the great and fragrant array of flourishing blooms: a regiment of cyclamens, each with its sweet white ears laid back; tulips, the vividness of whose varnished coats makes one wink; an army of cinerarias, each blossom a little scentless sun-disk of blazing colour; heavy bashful roses that set one dreaming of June. Poor, poor Joan! What will she do without her flowers? Poor little Joan!

As he thus kindly and pitifully addresses her, in his own soul, and mentally strokes her, she enters. The tall old door opens, and she comes in with a soft and dragging step. For so slender a thing she treads heavily, does not she? but sorrow puts leaden weights in one's feet. Wolferstan has hardly ever before seen her that she has not been either quite laughing, or else with unborn or half-born laughter hovering in the corners of her happy eyes. It is not that she has pulled a long face, even now, or is dressed in the mourner's airs, that some people, although truly sorrowing, think it right in such cases to wear.

She comes to meet him with a smile, but, alas! it has so clearly been put on only just outside the door, and is kept with such diffi-culty from brinily drowning itself. She looks half the size that he remembers her when last they parted, not that she ever was of the buxom sort. Hers was never one of your great luscious Rubens bodies, in whose depths of creamy flesh the poor little soul is oftenest lost and smothered. But now you can almost, as they say, see through her. One is always tenderly disposed towards thin people, though, in reality, they are not nearly such objects of compassion as the preposterously fat, towards whom no one's heart yearns.

Before he in the least knows what he is meaning to do (Wolferstan's actions mostly get ahead of his intentions), he is standing before her, holding both her hands; though the amount of their hitherto acquaintance would not justify more than the moderate shaking of one.

The trite and unconsoling consolations over which he laboured so heavily on his tree trunk depart to the limbo appointed for all abortions, and he finds himself saying hurriedly :

"Do you mind my coming ? do I bother you ? shall I go ?"

"No, don't !" she answers with a sort of eagerness, giving his hands a little unintentional squeeze of detention ; " it is good to

see some one! I was so glad when they
came and told me; I thought I never was
going to see any one again, and I have been
alone—alone—such a long time!" Her very
voice is changed: it sounds faint, and yet
hoarse, as if all its substance and sweetness
had been soaked away in tears. "This is a
bad house to be alone in, I can tell you," she
goes on in the same weak spent kind of tone,
lifting her eyes with a sort of relief to the
pity of his face; "you do not know how
ghostly the statues look at night—you have
only seen the gallery when it has been well
lit up; and the suits of armour are worse—
oh! far worse! last night I stared at them—
I could not help it—until I could have sworn
that there was a skeleton head under each
visor!"

She speaks the last words so low and
so quickly that he finds it hard to hear
them.

"Poor soul!" he says, taking both the chill
little hands, which are gradually growing

warmer in his close clasp, into one of his, in which they lie quite comfortably, and stroking their smooth backs with his freed one. " Why did not you send for me ?"

" That would have been so likely !" she says, with a little flash of maiden mirth struggling into her drowned eyes ; " if I had you would have thought that grief had unsettled my wits ! And not a soul has been near me," she continues presently, raising her voice a little, and speaking with slow emphasis, while her eyes still rest on his full and solemn, and with no more apparent consciousness in them of his being man, and herself woman, than if he had been the grandfather she deplores. " Not a soul ! except the doctor twice—he said both times that I was to keep up, and take a fizzing draught, and not think of anything disagreeable, and remember that everybody died—ha ! ha !—and the lawyer once——"

" Yes ; and what did he say to you ?" interrupts Wolferstan eagerly.

"He said—but why do you make me tell you? I see by your face that you know! there is not a hedger and ditcher about that does not know—he said, 'My dear young friend' (I never used to be his 'dear young friend!' I used to be 'Miss Dering,'" drawing up her little milk-white throat) "'my dear young friend, I am sorry that it has devolved upon me to be the bearer of ill tidings to you, but——'" (turning her head restlessly about like some poor dumb beast in physical pain), "'that I was a beggar in short,' those were not his words, of course; he said it much more lengthily and roundaboutly. I think he kept me on the rack for ten good minutes, but that was what it came to!"

"And was that all? did he tell you—did he say nothing else?" asks the young fellow with quick anxiety.

"*Was that all?*" she repeats with an almost angry emphasis, opening her eyes as widely as they will go; "was not that enough? Good Heavens! what else would you have had him say? what could be worse?"

Wolferstan does not answer aloud, but to his own heart he says "Thank God!"

"When he first told me," she goes on, as if speech were a relief, "I said I did not care a straw. I did not then; he thought it was bravado, but it was not; now I am beginning to care, dreadfully! it is enough to make any one care, is not it?"

"Merciful God! I should think it was!"

For a moment or two they stand silent, their position unaltered. It does not occur to them to sit down or to loose each other's hands. Sometimes, in trouble, the contact of warm human flesh is more comforting than any spoken words. And the sun comes in merrily, through the open window, and kisses them both, as not knowing which he likes best, and gives one stab more to the sick fire.

CHAPTER II.

"BUT how is it," resumes Wolferstan presently, harking back to her former speech, "that you say no one has been near you? Was not your uncle down here? they told me that he was."

"He came down here for the—the—I need not say it—you know," she answers, shying away with unconquerable repugnance from the grim word; "but he went away next day; and while he was here I did not see him—I would not: he is master here now, you know, and you may say that it was quarrelling with my bread-and-butter, but I could not; I stayed in my room; he never was at all kind or dutiful to *him*."

At the last words her voice altogether breaks, and snatching away both her hands from his, she covers all her small and woful face with them. It is perhaps as well; since otherwise he would probably have gone on holding them to the present day.

"You have heard all about it, I suppose?" she says after a pause, sitting listlessly down near the window, and pulling out of her pocket a pocket-handkerchief rather finer than a cobweb, and with an inky border a foot deep; according to our sensible fashion of making even our reluctant noses mourn our dead. "I suppose you saw it in the papers. I read the account of it in them all. I tried to fancy that it had nothing to say to me: there were two other sudden deaths in the *Times* on the same day—a young woman and a little child—I wondered how many people each of them had to be sorry for them: the worst part of crying," she says, with a slow and dragging accent, "is when one cries *alone*. I was the only person who cried for him."

Wolferstan looks down contritely. There is no earthly reason why he should have wept for old Squire Dering, and yet he would give fifty pounds to be able, truthfully, to tell her that he had shed tears for him. Even though, untruthfully, he would tell her so, only that he knows she would not believe him. He tries to mutter something to the effect that one may be very sorry for a thing without crying about it; but she goes on without paying the slightest heed to his well-meant mumble.

"Do you know," she says, leaning forward, and looking solemnly at him, "that only the evening before — after I had bidden him good-night, and was half-way upstairs to bed—something *drove* me back to have one other look at him? he was sitting, so" (resting one elbow on a little table near her, and pushing her fingers through her hair and

looking as unlike any old man as it is well
possible to look) "you know what beautiful
white hair he had—mine is coarse in comparison of it—and, young as you are, it was
as thick as yours! He asked me why I had
come back, and I could not say, I had no
reason!"

"Poor soul!"

Wolferstan is aware that he has said this
two or three times before, and would be glad
to vary it, did he know how, but there are
few ejaculations that hit the tepid medium
between the very much too warm and the
rather too cold.

"The next morning," she goes on, by-and-
by, with a long, low, sighing breath, "*the*
morning, you understand, I went out to the
Hall door to see him mount his horse, as I
always do—always *did*, I mean" (changing
the tense with a sort of sob), "and just as he
was riding away, he turned half round and
said, 'Go in, my Joan, this wind will cut
you in two!' those were the very last words

I ever heard him say! does not it seem odd"
(turning with awed yet puzzled appeal more
fully towards him) "that such a trivial speech
should be the very last I should have heard,
or ever shall hear now from him?" Then she
adds in a lower key, and more as a specula-
tion than a complaint, "Who will care how
the wind cuts me now, I wonder? No, don't
say that *you* will; it is very kind of you, but
it is nonsense! there is no reason why you
should!"

Again there is a silence, a longer one.
Wolferstan breaks it at last.

"And so you have to turn out of the old
house?" he says pityingly, casting his eyes
regretfully round him, looking up at the
painted ceiling, where water gods and sea
nymphs are frolicking, naked and unashamed,
in a sapphire sea; and then at the tapestried
walls, where gray-faced knights and leaden-
coloured ladies have been bowing and
parading and twanging guitars for the last
four hundred years.

"Yes," she answers, her eyes following his ; " and if my soul were to have to be torn out of my body, I think it could hardly be with a worse wrench ! There is to be a sale, you know," she goes on in a monotonous key of utter spiritlessness ; " my uncle hates the place : he is going to sell everything, even the pictures—think of that !—he says that his ancestors may go as cheap as Charles Surface's, for all he cares ! If I were not sure " (with a melancholy yet gracious smile) " that you had plenty of your own, I would ask you to buy them !"

" Shall I ?" he cries eagerly ; " I will bid for them with pleasure, if you like !" nor does he, in his compassionate readiness to saddle himself with all her forefathers, for one moment reflect on what he will do with the seventy or eighty odd Derings, when he has got them.

But she shakes her head, and says, " I was only joking !" Another pause. " You must not think," begins Joan again, finally drying

her poor eyes on the gossamer pocket-handkerchief, which is adapted neither for a great
grief nor a cold; "that I mean always to
go on moaning and whimpering like this : I
suppose it is seeing you that has set me off
again; else for three days—nearly four—I
have not shed a tear : I hoped I had come to
the end of them; there must be some end to
one's stock, must not there? and I think"
(drawing herself together, as one that nerves
himself for a hard struggle) "that I have
some little pluck about me somewhere, if I
could only come at it."

After an interval :

"Even if I could have had my own choice,"
she says, with a deep gravity, "I would not
always have been prosperous : I do not think
that the people who always have things their
own way are ever worth much; of course"
(shuddering) "I would not have chosen such
a trouble as this; but, after all, if one always
had smooth sailing, it could never be known
—one could never know oneself what sort of

stuff one was made of : I have a good chance
now of showing what sort of stuff I am made
of, have not I ?"

He looks at her with a compassion too
deep for words. He is always sorry for
every woman ; merely for being a woman,
and for being by this dismal accident debarred
from all the sinful and most of the unsinful
diversions of this life. His pity is centupled
in the case of this frail knight-errant going
out so valiantly in her paste-board armour to
battle with the great and ruthless dragon of
this bitter world.

" At least," she says, clenching one slight
hand, and looking upward, as one that
registers a vow ; " at least I will not be
knocked down by this first blow, like ripe
corn by a hail storm ! They have almost
explained away God nowadays, have not
they ?" she says, putting her hand in a sort
of bewildered way to her forehead ; " so
perhaps it is not He, but yet I feel that
there is something outside of me—something

not me—that will help me if I make a good fight!"

"You do not look as if it would take a very big blow to knock you down," he says sadly, looking at her with a deep commiseration, that is almost angry in its helplessness. For a moment he even wavers in his hitherto inviolable fidelity to fat women, as he notices how prettily and carelessly her slim young body lies in the great arm-chair into which she has thrown herself. It would hold three Joans.

"And yet," she answers, lifting her white lids, and considering his face awhile, full-eyed, with a quiet smile, as if taking his measure; "and yet perhaps—who knows?— a heavier one than would be needed to demolish you; it is not the bulky Samsons of this world that are the really strong ones: it is the small and wiry people, who, even if they are thrown down, are up again in a moment, and none the worse!"

"Am I a bulky Samson?" he asks, with a

half laugh; "if Samson were only five foot
eleven in his shooting boots, and rode only
thirteen stone, history has been very partial
to him!" A clock strikes; wrongly of course.
Who ever heard of a drawing-room clock with
a face looking out from amid a lovely flourish
of Dresden china flowers that told the hours
aright? But its voice, though a mistaken one,
reminds Wolferstan that there is such a thing
as time. "I have been here an hour," he
says, "and I meant to stay ten minutes; I
will go, but first—tell me—or, of course, if
you do not like, do not tell me—what your
plans are? with whom you will live? whither
you are going? I know that if I counted the
number of times that we have met, I should
find that 1 had no business to ask; but I will
not count. Tell me—what is going to become
of you?"

He has drawn much nearer to her, and is
again looking at her with the same over-
powering yet consciously-useless compassion.
As society stands, a young man is so very

powerless to help a young woman. To
marry her is the one doubtful kindness he
can show her: and marriage, as at present
constituted, does not find favour in Wolferstan's eyes.

"Do not be afraid!" she answers, with a
smile that, though sorrowful, is neither
cowardly nor broken-spirited. "I am not
going to the Workhouse, nor yet to the
Home for Lost Dogs or Decayed Gentle-
women; I am going to stay with an aunt of
mine—a sister of my mother's: though she is
my aunt, I have never seen her nor even
heard much about her. He never talked to
me about my mother's people."

She is looking at him, but he has turned
away his face, and is staring out of the
window.

"Did not he?" he answers rather indistinctly. A moment after: "An aunt? only
an aunt? no uncle?"

"He is dead."

"Any cousins?"

" I fancy so : she says something about the girls."

" Sons ?"

" I do not know ; I hope not : I dislike male cousins ; there is a sort of spurious brotherhood about them !"

" And you will make your home with this aunt ? will live with her ?"

" Until I can draw breath, and look about me."

He gives an impatient sigh, and a kick to a neighbouring foot-stool.

" Do not look so lamentable !" she says, almost laughing ; " it does sound deplorable, I own ; almost as bad as some of the cases in the Report of the Governesses' Institution ; no present income, no future prospects ! But, after all, it might be worse : since I am letting you into my private affairs, I may tell you that I have a thousand pounds that my godfather left me : that, at five per cent., will bring in fifty pounds a year ; one cannot positively starve on fifty pounds a year."

" Enough to buy one gown and perhaps a bonnet, you would have said a week ago."

" Yes," she answers, with a small but stifled sigh; " I must give up being fond of my clothes."

He shakes his head, as if to say that her affairs are beyond his mending.

" Well, in what part of the world am I to think of you, then ?" he says, with another sigh, reluctantly taking up his hat.

" I do not flatter myself that you will think of me much, in any part of the world," she says, a little dryly, and without any coquetry; though it is a sentence decidedly susceptible of a coquettish treatment; " but I shall be in Blankshire."

" My thoughts will have no long journey then ; that is my county : do you know what your post town is ?"

" It looks like Helmsley," she answers, drawing from her pocket a large and musky envelope, on which blazes a giant monogram, aflame with all the colours of the prism, and several more besides; "pah! how I hate patchouli! it has infected my pocket-handkerchief and all my other letters!"

"*Helmsley!*" he repeats, with a brightening of eye and alacrity of tone; "is that so, really? Then the plot is thickening: Helmsley is our post town too; we are not much more than three miles from it; what is your aunt's name? of course I must know her!"

"Her name is Moberley—Mrs. Moberley."

Wolferstan looks puzzled. "I know a Mrs. Moberley—at least—yes—I suppose I may be said to know her—certainly, quite as much of her as I ever wish to know—but *she* is not your aunt? ha! ha! I wish you could see her—it is odd!" (wrinkling his forehead, and putting one hand up to it as if to help his recollection); "but I thought I knew every living soul within a radius of ten miles of Helmsley. Moberley! Moberley!— how stupid of me!—can you tell me the name of her house?"

"Portland Villa," replies Joan, following the instinct which prompts us always to swallow three times as often as usual if we have a sore throat, and to turn our eyes a second time towards any disagreeable object which has accidentally regaled them, by smelling her aunt's letter again and making a face over it.

Wolferstan's jaw has dropped; in one second the complacence has died out of his face.

"Then it *is* the same!" he says in a low and awe-struck key; "but—you were joking! —she is not your aunt—it is impossible!—she cannot be!"

"But she is!" replied Joan, looking in some surprise at his aghast and discomfited features; "why should not she be? is she too young to have a niece?"

"And are the Miss Moberleys your *cousins*—your *first* cousins?" continues the young man, still speaking with a slow and horror-struck emphasis.

"Naturally! if she is my aunt and they are her daughters," says Joan a little tartly; "that is not a very hard sum to do."

"Gracious Heavens above us!"

"I wish," cries the girl, reddening a little, "that you would be more explicit and less ejaculatory; if you know anything very bad about them, please tell me directly! are they *mad?* have they done anything disgraceful?"

His face catches the flush from hers, but the emotion which expresses itself by the colour of a faint fine sunset on her cheeks is painted in full deep copper tints on his.

"You are making me very uncomfortable," she goes on after a moment's waiting, during which, bathed over head and ears in confusion, he is vainly struggling to overtake a speech which ever eludes him, "and it is not fair; you ought to tell me! is there anything odd about them?"

He tries to laugh in a stammering floundering fashion. "Odd! oh dear no! not that I know of!—upon my honour—please do not look as if you did not believe me—I—I— know nothing to their disadvantage; to tell the truth, I—I—you know I have been a great deal away from home—I—I—hardly know them : it was only that it—it—took me by surprise, don't you know ; it—it seemed unlikely."

Her sincere and straightforward eyes are looking directly at and through him; a small grain of half-amused pity steals into them, as he writhes and stutters before her.

"You might be making a speech at a wedding breakfast," she says sarcastically ; "I never heard anything so halting any- where else." After a thoughtful pause : "You said you 'wished I could see her,' why did you wish that I should see her? is she such a very remarkable sight?"

During the moment's breathing space of silence that she gave him, Wolferstan has been making some faintly prosperous efforts

to recover his countenance; but, at this
question, he has a frightful relapse. Thus,
brought face to face with his own words,
unable, beneath the honesty of her eyes, to
eat them, as he would otherwise be delighted
to do, he is too *ébahi* to attempt any answer
whatever. Joan looks away in pity from
his scarlet discomfiture. There is a pitch of
confusion which it makes one hot to witness,
and Wolferstan has reached it.

"I will ask you no more questions," she
says quietly. "I see that there is some
mystery, which I shall soon have the opportunity of fathoming. I suppose that she is
very odd - looking — ungainly? eccentric?
dowdy?" — stealing a covert glance at him
at each epithet, to see which epithet seems
to hit the right nail on the head. "Well, I
can forgive her for being any one of the three,
or even all three put together!" After a
pause: "Though you will not reveal anything about the *people*, you will not mind
telling me what sort of a place it is. Is it

a good house? are there nice gardens?—a
pretty park?"

Wolferstan opens his eyes. "I do not
think that there is much *park*," he answers
slowly; "it is not exactly the sort of place
where one expects a park; it is not a large
house, you know; in fact—well—a small one!
—and it is not very far from—indeed, rather
close to—the road."

He makes these admissions as if they
were being dragged out of him by hot
pincers.

"About how small?" asks Joan seriously,
as she mentally tries to cut and pare down
her ideas to the right size. He looks up at
the distant ceiling, and round at the wide
walls.

"I think the whole of it would pretty
nearly go into this room!"

Despite her heartiest efforts her face
lengthens a little.

"It must be a *hovel*," she says in a low
voice; then, resolutely pulling herself together

again : "It is no great matter," she says steadily ; "there is something cosy about a small house ; there is no hardship in being shut up in a narrow space with nice people— and they *are* nice" (looking resolutely at him, and speaking with a determined emphasis) —"I *know* they are nice ; no one that was not nice could have written this —" (again glancing at the ill-savoured missive she holds in her hand). "A letter of condolence is a good test."

He says neither yea nor nay ; he has already taken up his hat, and has been in the agonies of going for the last five minutes. Now he puts out his hand. "Good-bye," he says, looking at her with a grave and undissembled regret, and—which is not alto-gether usual with him—neither saying nor looking any more than he thoroughly means ; "it is not quite so bad to say 'good-bye,' now that I know for certain that we shall soon shake hands again ; and meanwhile send me a line, will not you ?—' Guards' Club' will always find me—if I can do anything for you."

" It is not a very likely ' if,'" she answers gently. " No—henceforth no one is to do anything for me. The new régime has begun : I am to do everything for myself. I am even learning to dress my own hair ; see—it is not so bad !—and when you come to see me at Portland Villa, you will find it better still. Good-bye."

She is smiling, but her eyes are wet : the tears indeed have over-brimmed, and are dropping down her white and fine - grained cheeks.

And so he leaves her. As he walks back the church bells are dumb, and he neither whistles nor sings. He has lost two grandfathers himself in his day, with grandmothers to match, and borne it like a Trojan. But this is different. He feels as if his hour's stay within those gray walls had made him a soberer sadder man. But we are creatures of habit ; and that very same evening sees him again squeezing his old friend's fingers under the candlestick ; indeed, as she is now prepared for the manœuvre, and not unwilling, he finds himself in temporary possession of her whole hand !

CHAPTER III.

ES! the new régime has begun. No one beyond childhood is fond of a new order of things merely because it is new. Everybody hates new boots; most people hate new situations.

On most ears the joy bells of New Year's Eve, rashly and over-hastily mirthful, jar. Why, in Heaven's name, should we pull bells and get drunk because we are one twelve-month nearer "the Conqueror Worm"? If it were the worm that rang the bells we could understand his jollity.

Joan's new régime, over which she has

about as much reason to exult as we over
our new year, may be said to begin as she
steams out of the station at Dering, with
the footman standing on the platform, and
touching his hat to her for the last time.
She tried to inaugurate the new epoch
last night, when she made a zealous effort to
pack her own clothes ; and after hours of
patient but unskilled wrestling rose from before the imperials, which indignantly dis-
gorged her too numerous gowns—rose fagged
and red, yet semi-triumphant under the idea
that at least she had succeeded in getting
everything in—only to discover behind her a
forgotten and overlooked heap, hardly inferior in size and incompressibility to that
with which she has been contending. There-
upon the old régime returns for the moment,
and her maid, who has been looking on in impatient pain at dresses folded in the wrong
places—at vacuums where no vacuums should
be—and a general inartistic inequality of level,
retakes her office and for the last time packs.

When all her imperials—great and many, as if she were an American—are at length shut, locked, and strapped, Joan eyes them with a new distrust.

"If the house is as small as he said, they will never get into it!"

Joan has no good-bye kisses to give, at least not to people. She kisses a chair, a walking-stick, a pair of muffetees that she herself had knitted only two months ago; but they do not kiss her back again, and one-sided kissing is, as every one knows, a discouraging employment. She cannot even kiss the fresh spring grass that grows above her grandfather's head, for no fresh green grass does grow above it. He lies far down in a great and peopled vault—the Dering mausoleum, on the building of whose solid gruesomeness some bygone Dering spent a fortune. It would be small comfort to Joan to go inside the high-spiked iron railings, and give her forlorn good-bye kiss to the great stone slabs that cover the entrance. It would be given to twenty others as much as to him.

The journey that is before her is long, so she sets off early. For the last time she opens her eyes on a lace-edged pillow, and looks round at her dainty walls, palely hung in shimmering green, at her toilette table, at the cheval glass in which she has so often seen and so thoroughly enjoyed the sight of the reflection of her own figure and Worth's gowns.

The thought just passes through her head: " In what sort of a room shall I wake to-morrow?" but she dismisses it. " What does it matter ?"

For the last time she drinks her coffee out of a canary-coloured cup, with little ladies and gentlemen making love upon it in the easy, sunshiny, practical way in which china love is always made—a cup so thin and transparent that you hardly feel it between your lips as you sip. For the last time she is carried to the station on C. springs, drawn through the first sharp freshness of a young April morning by a pair of satin-coated bays, tightly bearing-reined, and loftily stepping over their own noses.

You will say that there is nothing affecting in these "last times," that if she were parting for the last time with a sweetheart—exchanging with him split rings or crooked sixpences—you could be sorry for her, but not now. And yet he could be much more easily and cheaply replaced than can satin hangings or bay thoroughbreds.

For the last time the footman gets her her ticket, for the first and last time (this is perhaps the exact moment when the new life opens and the old one closes) he tells her in which van he has put her boxes—hitherto in all her former travels this has been no concern of hers.

With one ear-piercing yell, as of a lost soul, the train is off, and with a parting view of the footman and of all the porters looking rather relieved at having one more of the

morning trains off their minds, Joan is off
too. Past quite familiar fields first—*his*
fields, where she seems to know every hedge-
row thorn, every pasturing cow as well as
she knows all the little dips and pleasant
rises in the park, where the very sunshine and the skittish winds seem to belong
specially to the Derings; then past farms
and wheat-fields and rickyards less familiar;
then quite strange.

Joan longs to cry. What do sore-hearted
dogs do—dogs who cannot cry—into the
wistfulness of whose sorrowful eyes no tears
can steal, and yet who have quite as much
capacity for the sufferings that the affections
cause as any Niobe that ever wept herself to
stone? But Joan can cry, and thanks God
for it. The tears are already dripping one
after another, quick and large, on her crape
lap, when all inclination to weep is suddenly
and effectually choked and killed by the dis-
covery that, on the seat opposite to her, a
child is deposited—a fat, crêpé-haired, pros-

perous child—who is staring at her with
unblinking brazen pertinacity; in solemn
astonishment that a grown-up person can
cry. Then her tears seem dried and burnt
up at their fountain; she puts her pocket-
handkerchief back into her pocket, feeling
sure that she will no longer need it.

It is perhaps as well. One must stop crying some day, and this day, Monday, April
12th, is perhaps as good as any other. It is
as difficult to weep in a train with a person
opposite looking at you, as it is to eat sand-
wiches gracefully and comfortably under the
like circumstances. By-and-by, finding that
Joan furnishes no further phenomena for
observation, the child slithers down from its
seat, and begins to run playfully up and down
the carriage upon the inmates' feet. Then it
climbs up again on the seat and thrusts most
of its body out of the open window, excluding
air and view; being forcibly pulled down
and re-seated by a palpitating parent, it
screws up its nose and howls.

Joan's is a long and weary journey, and there are many changes. The ticket that the footman got her does not last her for the whole length; she has to get another for herself. It is market-day, and for some other and unexplained reason there are more people than usual travelling. She has to stand— one of a long string of people—before the ticket-office, with a heated market-woman before her, and a high-flavoured hurried man treading on her gown, thrusting her on, and roughly urging her to be quick in taking up her change, behind her.

She forgets in which van her luggage was put. She is nearly knocked down by a porter and truck trundling noisily down the platform, inexorable as Destiny and as unalterable in their course. The other porters are over-worked and unkind, and have quite laid aside their usual suavity. The attention of most of them is occupied by a furious man-passenger, who has lost his portmanteau and is dealing death and damnation round to the whole staff in consequence. When at length, by dint of painful perseverance, she has induced one of them to give her his reluctant attention, she finds that his whole soul revolts against the number and magnitude of her boxes.

His sense of fitness is evidently jarred by finding that a single woman travelling ignobly alone, without maid or footman or male protector, and who, by all the laws of analogy and probability, should have been contented with one modest canvas-covered box and a carpet-bag, is furnished with an array of imperials that would not disgrace a countess.

From a conscientious desire to economise, she travels the last half of her journey second-class. The carriage is at first full, gorged to repletion with market-people who crowd in in much greater number than the carriage can hold, and jocosely sit upon each other's knees. They gradually diminish, as each station drains a few off, and she is at length left *tête-à-tête* with one man, distinctly drunk, who insists on shaking hands with her when he too, at last, to her infinite relief, gets out. When at length (to her it seems a very long length) the train draws up at Helmsley station, she is alone.

It is evening; well on towards night, indeed, and the station lamps gleam all a-row. Having got out, she stands looking wistfully about to see whether she can notice any one that looks as if they had come to meet her. In vain. The station is rather empty; there is no one that looks the least expectant, or is eying with any air of possible proprietorship any of the men or women that the train is disburdening itself of. Work being tolerably slack the porters are able to attend to her. In process of time—it takes time—all her great boxes stand on the platform.

" Where to ? please, ma'am."

" I suppose that they must have sent to meet me," she answers uncertainly. "Do

you know if there is a carriage here ? Mrs.
Moberley's carriage ?"

" What name did you say, 'm ?"

" Moberley — Mrs. Moberley," speaking
with painstaking distinctness.

He shakes his head.

" Do not know any one of that name ; Jim,
run and see whether there's a carriage a-
waiting."

In two minutes Jim is back.

" There ain't no carriage of any kind."

A disheartened chill creeps over Joan.
They have neither come nor sent.

" There is no cart for the luggage then,
either, of course ?"

" No, there ain't no cart neither."

" I must hire a fly then, I suppose," she
says, swallowing a sigh. " *Will* one fly take
them all ? if not, I must have two flies."

" There ain't no flies here, 'm," replies the
porter suavely ; " unless you order them
aforehand."

" No flies !" repeats Joan, eyes and mouth

both opening in utterest discomfiture; "then how *am* I to get there?"

"They keep a fly at the Railway Inn, 'm," says Jim, who is younger and tenderer hearted than his comrade. "You can have that if it is not out."

"And where is the Railway Inn?" she asks, catching at this straw, and with a faint gleam of comfort dawning on her soul. "Is it near?"

"Just over the way, 'm," he answers, pointing across the line to the other side of the station; "not more nor a hundred yards off."

"Will you go and order it for me then, please?" she cries eagerly; "tell them to get it ready at once—as soon as ever they can!" (lapsing unintentionally into the tones of polite authority and command that have been habitual to her all her life).

"If it is in, 'm; but it is mostly out."

With this cold comfort he leaves her. She sits down on the smallest of her boxes, with a weighty dressing-case, that makes her knees ache, on her lap. She looks vacantly round : first at an engine that is fussing and snorting about by itself ; then at a man who is shutting up the bookstall ; then through the doors of the glaring refreshment-room at the giant-headed young ladies and commercial travellers exchanging gallantries. By-and-by her emissary comes back.

"Please, 'm, it is out !"

"*Out !*"

She has not faced this possibility, though he has warned her of its likelihood. It seemed one of those things that are too bad to be true.

"It took a party up to Brickhill this afternoon, and it ain't back yet ; they do not expect it back for another couple of hours !"

"Then what *am* I to do ?" says Joan, still sitting on her box, and speaking with slow desperation.

She does not mean it as a question put to

the porter, but more as an ejaculation, a protest addressed to destiny—to nature—to the dumb distant sky, where all the nightly fires are beginning to be lit. But he takes it to himself.

" Perhaps, 'm, if you would step across and speak to Mr. Smith yourself—it is he as keeps the Railway Inn."

" I will," she says, catching at the suggestion ; " thank you."

And so rises, and staggers across the line as quickly as the weight of her dressing-case will let her.

" Just oppo-*site*, 'm," says the porter, leaning heavily and lengthily on the last syllable of the word, accompanying her outside the station and pointing. " You cannot miss it !"

Then he goes and leaves her alone in the world.

Oh, why—oh, why did not he stay and escort her ? But he spoke truth. She cannot miss it. " Railway Inn " in gilt letters across

the wall ; " Railway Inn" in gilt letters across
the blinds. It " tells its name to all the hills,"
as plainly as Wordsworth's cuckoo. About
the door stand a knot of men enjoying bad
tobacco, starlight, and small beer, and before
the door stands a butcher's cart, whose master
has evidently just pulled up to refresh himself.

They all take their pipes out of their mouths,
and stop talking as she approaches. Joan has
entered a score of well-thronged drawing-
rooms, has made her curtsy to her Sovereign
and danced with her Sovereign's sons, with a
good deal less nervousness than she now experiences in introducing herself to this half-
dozen of convivial boors.

" I am sorry to hear that your fly is out,"
she says abruptly, and looking from one to
the other, as not knowing to which her question belongs.

" Yes, miss, it is ; it took a party to Brickhill this——"

" I know," she answers, interrupting ; " and

have you no other conveyance? no wagonette?
no dog-cart?"

"I 'ave a dog-cart, miss, but you see my
son has took it to market to Ongar this
morning, and he's oftenest not back afore ten
or eleven!"

What camel's back could stand such a last
straw as this? Were it not for the audience
Joan would put down her dressing-case in the
dusty road, would sit upon it, and break into
forlorn weeping. As it is, she only looks
round rather pitifully; for they are not drunk,
and seem quite ready to be civil and sorry,
and says, sighing patiently:

"Then I must walk; do you think you
could help me to find a boy to carry *this*, it is
very heavy; I do not think that I could carry
it for three miles, and I believe that that is
the distance."

"If you please, miss, which direction is it
you are going in?" asks a man who has not
spoken hitherto; a man with a purple nose,
a husky voice, and one of those blue blouses

that all oxen, calves, and sheep must regard
with so lively a distrust and aversion.

"I am afraid that I do not know even
that," she answers, turning to this new inter-
locutor, and speaking with a starved little
smile. "I only know the name of the house,
and the name of the lady to whom it belongs
— Portland Villa — Mrs. Moberley — Mrs.
Moberley—Portland Villa!" laboriously re-
peating and elaborating each syllable.

"Po-ortland Villa!" repeats he dubiously;
"you do not happen to know, miss, which
side of the town it is on? they've been
building a many new villas lately. Bill, do
you know where Po-ortland Villa is?"

Bill shakes his head. He does not know.
None of them know. Portland Villa is
apparently not much known to fame.

"I should not wonder," suggests the landlord presently, "if it were one of them
houses on the London Road; little houses
with a bit of garden at the back, about three
miles out of the town; just after you pass

the Cancer 'Orspital and afore you come to
the Lunatic Asylum."

Joan shudders. Good Heavens ! What a
situation !

"If that is your road, miss," says the
husky butcher affably, "why it is mine too ;
I can give you a lift as far as the 'Orspital ;
it won't take me none out of my way."

"You are very good," answers Joan, not
yet quite taking in the situation ; "thank you
very much ; you are going to drive in that
direction ?"

He nods towards the cart, and the stout
gray horse, who, with his nose in a bag, is
waiting with the good-humoured patience
engendered by long habit outside in the starlight.

"That is my cart, miss, and I don't mind
giving you a ride in it."

She gives a little unintentional gasp, but
happily nobody notices it. It is not often,
perhaps, that it has happened to a lady to
drive in the morning to a station in a

barouche, behind a pair of sleek thoroughbreds, and with a six-foot London footman to
open the door for her: and to drive *from* a
station in the evening in a butcher's cart.
However, it is butcher's cart or nothing, so
she chooses the former. Not being used to
mounting into carts, and being tired and
rather faint, she shows no great agility, and
a chair is brought out to aid her. By its
help she clambers in, and her dressing-case
is solemnly handed up after her. It is the
first time that it also has travelled in a
butcher's cart. Once seated, she looks
apprehensively round to see whether any
dismembered calf or murdered lamb is to be
her companion. The butcher apparently
divines her fears.

"Quite empty, miss," he says reassuringly; "there ain't no jints!" Then he
takes a stirrup cup from the fair hand of an
easy-mannered barmaid, strips off the nose-
bag, climbs in without a chair, shakes the
reins, crying "Tcl!" and they are off.

For the first few minutes, Joan is entirely occupied by the novelty of her sensations. She wonders how soon she will turn a somersault backwards over the backless bench. It seems to her only a question of time. And then how it shakes! The treatment that a physic bottle experiences appears to her gentle in comparison of that to which she is subjected. She feels as if all her vital organs were getting hopelessly mixed and entangled together. Joan has hitherto only seen life from the boxes or stalls. She is now beginning to learn how engaging it can look from the upper galleries. It is a fair meek night, not very light, for not all the million little stars can make up for the absence of the one great moon; but yet a very gentle twilight, by which lovers might kiss, and friends softly talk. The station is a mile distant from Helmsley town: by-and-by they are jolting and clattering over the streets; cabs and carriages pass them: lamp-posts hold up their yellow lights to out-twinkle the white

stars : people are walking along the *trottoir* ;
dirty girls, idle soldiers, staring into such
shops as are still open; policemen. Then
out of the town again, along a road that is
neither a road nor yet a street—a melancholy
hybrid—dreary as only the outskirts of a
town can be. Just begun houses—half-
finished houses, with the poles of their
scaffoldings gauntly cutting the sky ; heaps
of bricks. She shudders with a feeling of
disheartened repulsion, saying to herself in
heart sickness, " Is it possible that it can be
here ?" But fate is not quite so unkind.
Farther still; till the country begins to be
almost country again ; till the fields grow
grass instead of bricks ; till the trees are trees
with leafy crowns instead of naked scaffolding poles. A large building in all the harsh-
ness of utter squareness is lifting itself before
their eyes ; sulkily out-lined against the
pensive night. Her companion pulls up.

" This is the 'Orspital, miss."

Again she shudders. What a ghastly and

ominous finger-post to point her to her destination.

"'That is your road, miss" (pointing with his whip). There is no chair to help her this time; so she scrambles down as best she can.

"No obligation at all, miss! I wish you good-night."

The old gray is in a hurry, apparently; for he is off before she can make up her mind as to whether his master would be insulted by being offered a tip or no. She is left standing alone in the middle of the road. It is very still—very silent. There is not a passer-by; no smallest sound hits the ear. There is no light save what the stars give, and a dull red glimmer from two or three of the windows of the great Lazar House beside her. What if she have been misled by a wrong information? what if Portland Villa do not lie in this direction at all? What will she do then? She will have to beg for a night's lodging at the 'Orspital.

With a heart beating hard and quick from fear, and sick and weary with inanition, she hastens, as quickly as the weight that she has to carry will let her, towards the indicated goal. Four mean little detached houses (even by this flattering star-light she can see that they are mean) lie ahead of her; each seated in its garden plot; each with its own small carriage drive and stone posted entrance gates. She reaches the first, and ravenously reads the name that, painted in black letters, adorns the gate-posts : " Sardanapalus Villa !" On to the next : " De Cressy Villa !" The third : " Campidoglio Villa !" There is only one more. For a moment she dares not look. Too much hangs on the issue of that glance. For a moment she looks in the other direction : then gathering up her courage, turns her eyes upon the fateful posts : " Portland Villa !"

CHAPTER IV.

" The little dogs and all,
Tray, Blanche, and Sweetheart, see they bark at me !"

T is not quite easy to make out the name at a glance, from the fact that, through lack of a renewal of paint the P has nearly disappeared. Still, enough of it remains to prove that it once was there; enough to make Joan's sunk spirits rise again with a leap.

It is right, then! It is Portland Villa, at last. The landlord's instructions were correct. She puts out her hand to unlatch the gate; only to discover that it is off its hinges, and

—to remedy this defect—is tightly tied up
with string. She sets down her dressing-
case in the road ; while her fingers struggle
to untie the manifold hard knots which
guard the entrance to Mrs. Moberley's
bower.

While she is thus employed she hears a
scampering of many little feet on the gra-
velled drive, and from the house rushes forth
a volley of dogs, one over another. There
seem to be twenty at least ; but subsequent
counting reduces them to six : all smallish ;
all, apparently, deeply warmly hostile ; all
barking with a deafening volubility ; all
breathing wrath and indignation against the
profane intruder who is tampering with their
entrance gates at ten o'clock at night. Their
harmony accompanies her all the time that
she is struggling with the knots. They also
make it doubtful to her whether the bell
which she has pulled on reaching the door
has really rung. They bark themselves
nearly off their own legs ; and if there were

any dead in the neighbourhood, would infallibly wake them.

But their conversation has changed in tone. It no longer means enmity so much as excitement, agitation, half-welcome. Having smelt her clothes to be good and genteel, they have convinced themselves that in such a gown she cannot be come begging. Anyhow, theirs is the only welcome she seems likely to get; for, whether the bell rang or no, it is certain that nobody answers it. She rings again, and again waits. Nothing happens. Can it be the wrong day? Is it possible that they are all out?—even the servants; and that this army of little dogs is keeping house alone?

She pulls out her aunt's letter from her pocket, and tries to decipher it by the starlight. " Monday, April 12th," as plain as Charles' Wain above her head. If there be a mistake it is not hers. Emboldened by this fact she rings a third time. After a considerable interval—not of silence, for the six dogs do not permit that, but of patient,

dispirited waiting—she hears a slow and
solid foot coming along the passage inside.
A bolt is withdrawn; the door opens; a flood
of light flows out from a lit hall, and a person
—a female person — appears in the aper-
ture.

"I suppose that Mrs. Mob—" begins Joan,
then stops, for some lightning-quick intuition
tells her that—wildly improbable as it seems
—*this* is Mrs. Moberley.

"Why, *I* am Mrs. Moberley, my dear,"
says that lady, putting out both hands and
drawing the girl in with them. "I did not
think it could be you because I did not hear
any wheels : to tell you the truth, I think I
must have been having forty winks. Hold
your tongues, dogs! get away, Regy! get
away, Algy! get away, Charlie! get away,
Mr. Brown!"

During this speech Miss Dering is regarding her aunt with an intensity of gaze, hardly
compatible with her usual good manners; but,
indeed, it is difficult to look at Mrs. Moberley

on a first introduction in any other way than intensely.

Mrs. Moberley is certainly startlingly fat; but so you may say are many ladies, who, having outlived the thinning excitements of girlhood, take life easily; relish their food, and lapse without much difficulty into slumber. But Mrs. Moberley's is not that tight, compact, well-busked fat which, to one class of mind, is not without its attractiveness. Hers is of the unsteady order that destroys all land marks and laughs at boundary lines. Mrs. Moberley is absolutely without any shape at all.

"I do not know what Sarah can be thinking of not to have answered the bell!" she goes on, as she recloses the door and refastens the bolt; "but I suspect the fact is, that she is at her supper; and, as I always say to the girls, it is my belief that if the last trump were to sound while she was at her supper, she would wait till she had finished before she would attend to it—ha! ha!" Her very laugh is fat. If your eyes were shut you could swear that it had not proceeded from a slight person.

Joan is speechless. She is thinking that she no longer wonders at Wolferstan's wish that she could see her aunt. Certainly she is well worth seeing.

"But where are your things, child? what have you done with your luggage?" continues Mrs. Moberley, recovering from her mirth, and preparing to reopen the door; "are they outside?"

"I had to leave them at the station; I could not get a fly—there was not one."

"No fly!" repeats her aunt in high and staccato accents of astonishment; "why what had become of the fly from the Railway Inn? they have a very good fly there—quite a smart one: the girls always say that you could not tell it from a private carriage at a little distance."

"It was out."

"And — you — walked — all—the—way?

Three miles and a half if it is a step"
(opening her eyes as widely as the encroach-
ments of her cheeks will let her).

" No, I did not," replies Joan, with a hys-
terical laugh, for she has eaten but one bun
all day, is faint and most weary, and it is so
much worse than she had expected. " I
came in a butcher's cart as far as the Cancer
Hospital."

" In a butcher's cart!" (lifting up hands
and eyes). " This will be a fine story for the
girls : I am afraid they will never let you
hear the last of it. I wonder"—in a tone of
quickened interest —" was it our butcher ?
You did not happen to notice the name on
the cart, did you ?"

" I never thought of looking," replies Joan,
still struggling with a most painful inclination
to laugh violently and cry violently at the
same moment.

" I do not think that he could have been
yours though ; he did not seem to know you
when I mentioned your name."

"In a butcher's cart!" repeats Mrs. Moberley, still chuckling with fat relish; "it was lucky it was night, was not it? people would have stared to see a stylish girl like you perched up in a butcher's cart, would not they?"

All this time they have been in the passage; but now Mrs. Moberley puts her arm round her niece; first giving her several hearty kisses, and begins to lead her towards the interior of the bower. But the passage is narrow; and on peril of becoming wedged between the walls, they have to part company and enter the drawing-room in single file.

Joan had thought that her heart was already so low down that it would be impossible to abase it any farther, but the sight of the drawing-room undeceives her. It is not that it is shabby, though it is that too in a very high degree, but there are many worse things in this world than shabbiness. It is the air of slip-shod finery about it which so utterly capsizes the poor remnant of Joan's spirits. A white paper, freely starred with large (once gold) heavenly bodies ; many ornaments of a shelly sparry nature, inexpensively florid : an impression of much cheap pink ribbon and gobble-stitch lace ; and—though the month is wealthy April—not a flower, with the exception of a giant bunch of artificial ones under a glass shade.

"This is the drawing-room !" says Mrs. Moberley, introducing it with an air of pleased proprietorship ; "we have not laid out much money upon it, for the excellent reason that we have not had much to lay—ha ! ha ! but the girls have managed to make it look pretty smart too, have not they ?"

"They have indeed," replies Joan emphatically, looking round with a rather moon-struck air, and taking in many details of wool, of beads, of red Bohemian glass, which at the first *coup d'œil* had escaped her notice.

"In a butcher's cart," repeats Mrs. Moberley, again resuming her chuckle, and sinking down into a chair in order the more luxuriously to enjoy it ; "it really is the richest thing I ever heard ! The girls meant to have gone and met you to-day—they had put their hats on, on purpose—when—who should come in but Micky—Micky Brand, you know—or, rather, of course, you do not know—and whisked them off to tea at the Barracks !"

" Yes ?"

Her eyes have strayed to the dogs, who, now silent, and consenting to her adoption into the family, are sitting all six in a row, very close together before the low fire, and occasionally overcome by sleep, falling against each other.

" He—would—not—take ' no,' " continues Mrs. Moberley slowly ; " he is so droll, is Micky ; a vast deal of dry humour about him ! I am sure that you and he will get on like a house on fire : I can see that you are just the sort of girl he will take to at once."

" Am I ?" (with a sickly little smile).

Joan is angry with herself for being so monosyllabic, but her tongue refuses to frame any words longer than " yes " or " no." There is one monosyllabic word, indeed, which her whole soul is crying aloud, but her lips do not venture to utter it, and that word is "tea!"

"He is in the 170th, you know," pursues Mrs. Moberley, warming with her theme. "I did not mention to you in my letter that Helmsley was a garrison town; I thought it would be a little surprise for you!" She is looking at her with such an air of good-natured expectancy as she makes this exciting revelation that Joan is really and honestly sorry that she cannot look more exhilarated by it. "A regiment is the making of a country place, is not it?" continues her aunt complacently; "and these are a very dashing set of fellows, they keep us all alive!"

Joan is saved from the necessity of answering a question to which she feels so incapable of making a satisfactory response, by the behaviour of the dogs, who, in a moment, are all awake, and on their legs; barking again

with hardly less violent unanimity than that
with which they greeted Miss Dering.

"Hold your tongues, dogs!" cries Mrs.
Moberley; "hold your tongue, Mr. Brown!
you are always the ringleader!" But small
heed pays Mr. Brown. With one flying leap
he is out of the window, followed by his five
brothers and sisters; and all are barking their
hearts out at their ease in the starlight. "It
is the girls!" explains Mrs. Moberley; "and,"
with a look of pleased alertness, "I think I
hear a man's voice too, do not you? I believe
it is Micky; he said he should very likely
come to make his bow to you, but I took it
for a joke."

By this time the dogs' clamour is hushed.
They are evidently apologising for their mistake.

"Do not go yet!" cries a high young voice
outside; "it is quite early! come in and have
some brandy and soda-water!"

"Do not offer what you have not got," cries
Mrs. Moberley, raising her voice, and laugh-

ingly calling through the window ; " there is no soda-water in the house !"

" I modify my invitation then," replies the young voice ; " come in and have some brandy without the soda-water !" (laughing also).

But this Bacchanalian offer is apparently declined ; for, after a few seconds of further parley, carried on in too low a key to be overheard, the Miss Moberleys enter the house and the room alone.

" What have you done with Micky ?" cries their mother eagerly. "Why did not you bring him in ?"

" He would not come," replies one of the girls ; " he said he had not time ; but we think that it was because he had his mess-jacket on —he knows that it is not becoming !"

" Evidently anxious to make a good impression at first sight !" says Mrs. Moberley ; and they all laugh—all but Joan.

Mirth is indeed far from Miss Dering's thoughts. At the present moment she is

occupied in gazing at her two first cousins
with hardly less intensity than that which
marked her first view of their mother. And
yet they are of no uncommon type. Had
she seen them officiating in the Helmsley
refreshment-room, or behind the counter at
the fancy repository in the little town near
Dering, she would have passed them without
an observation. It is as *first cousins—her*
first cousins that they strike her as so as-
tounding. First cousins ! in such hats ! such
jackets ! such earrings ! such beads ! and with
such a trolloping length of uncurled curls
down their backs ! Had you told her that
Mr. Brown and Algy were her first cousins, it
would have seemed to her less surprising.

"I daresay you do not know which is
which !" says Mrs. Moberley, following the
direction of her niece's eyes, and regarding
her progeny with a contained pride. "I
daresay you are trying to make out which is
Bell, and which is Di, without my telling you.
Do you see much likeness between them ?"

she goes on a moment later, as Joan still maintains a stupefied silence ; "some say they might be twins, others do not see it. I suppose," with a good-natured glance round the room, comprehensively inclusive—" I suppose there is a family look among us all."

"We are not at all alike really," cries the younger, least beaded, least vivid-looking of the two girls, in an anxious voice ; "if we seem so at first, it goes off after a while."

"I am sorry we were not back in time to receive you," says the other, sitting down and taking off her hat. "Diana and I meant to have gone to meet you ; we were just setting off when—mother has told you ?—he came on purpose—he gave us no peace !"

"I daresay you were very glad," says Diana bluntly. "We should have crowded you up ; I daresay that there was not more than enough room for you and your boxes in the fly ?"

"The fly indeed !" cries Mrs. Moberley, beginning to laugh again ; "a fine fly. It is evident that they are not in the secret. Is not it, Joan?"

At the sound of her own Christian name (and after all what else is her own aunt likely to call her?) Joan gives a slight and involuntary shudder, but it passes harmless and unobserved amid the fire of question, answer, ejaculation, and retort that now ensues.

"You must have passed us on the road," says Bell, presently. "Did you notice? we were walking two and two; Diana and Micky in front, and I and another officer behind: we did not see you, but then"—laughing affectedly—"you were in the very last place where we should ever have thought of looking for you."

"Did it jolt very badly?" asks Diana, fixing upon her cousin's small wan face a pair of honest and very well-opened eyes, filled with compassionate inquiry; "worse than a 'bus? were you much shaken? you look so tired!" The genuine rough pity of her tone goes nigher to upsetting Miss Dering than all her former discomfitures. The tears rush to her eyes.

"It has been a long day," she says, faltering. "I set off early!"

"And have you had nothing to eat?" cries Diana, turning her quick eyes round the room in search of those signs of conviviality which are conspicuous by their absence; "no tea? nothing?" Then, as Joan observes an embarrassed silence, she goes on—her healthy cheeks flushing a little: "There is never much to eat or drink in this house, and what there is, is not at all appetising, but at least we can give you some tea."

So saying, she hastily leaves the room. It is some time—to Joan it seems a very long time—before she returns. At length, however, she reappears, bearing in her hands a tray, and with a face so very much heightened and deepened in tint as sufficiently proves that she herself has been the cook.

"The servants had gone to bed," she says apologetically; "the fire was nearly out, and

the kettle would not boil. Come, Joan",
eying rather ruefully the sorry fare—" I am
sorry that there is nothing more inviting, but
it is the best we have."

Joan obeys, nothing loth. The tea is very
weak and rather smoky, and it is clear that
one need go no farther than an English hedge
for its original home ; the bread is very stale
and the butter very salt ; but to a person who,
within the last twenty-four hours, has re-
freshed herself with but one cup of coffee
and one bun, few drinks do not seem to
be nectar, few viands do not taste succu-
lently.

It is a long, long while after Miss Dering
has come to the end of her meagre refreshment before the idea of going to bed presents
itself to the minds of Mrs. Moberley or her
daughters. At last, at last—a very long
last—and when Joan can no longer hinder
her tired head from sinking forward on her
breast in uncomfortable jerky slumber, there
comes a lull—a talk of going to bed, a dawd-

ling chattering preparation for carrying the
idea into execution, and lastly a lighting of
candles.

"Good-night, Joan," says her aunt, holding both her hands and looking at her with
good-natured eyes, which evidently once were
large, but which now, through the dis-
honest usurpation by her checks of territory
not belonging to them, are decidedly small.
"I hope we shall see some more red in these
cheeks to-morrow. Your mother used to
have such a fine colour, quite as high as
Bell's, if not higher; often and often people
have asked me if she were not painted." A
moment later: "Do not trouble to get up to
breakfast to-morrow, child; we often do not—
we never have any particular breakfast hour
—only just as any of us feel inclined. This
is Liberty Hall, my dear—Liberty Hall."
So saying she looses her niece's little chill
hands, and, nodding her head several times,
disappears into her bower, while Joan,
escorted by her two cousins, drags her weary

legs up the narrow deal staircase of "Liberty Hall."

"This is your room," says Diana, throwing open a door and waving her flat candlestick about, so as to exhibit its dimensions, "the guest-chamber of *Liberty Hall*," with a little sarcastic mimicking of her mother's tone. "I will not say that I hope you will find it comfortable, because I know you will not."

"There is a bed," answers Joan, with a small smile of utter weariness; "that seems to me the only thing of the least importance just now."

But if she imagines that this broad hint will rid her of the company of her relations she is greatly mistaken. Diana sets down the candle, and Arabella seats herself upon a cane-bottomed chair. To hide her disappointment Joan walks to the window.

"You have the best view in the house," says Arabella complacently; "you can see everything that goes along the road better even than from the drawing-room."

But it is air, not view, that Miss Dering craves. The room feels close and confined. She throws up the sash, which instantly and clamorously falls down again.

" It always does that," says Arabella composedly; "there has been something odd about it for months. It keeps open pretty well with a bit of wood; there generally is a bit of wood, but of course Sarah has lost it."

She sets the candlestick on the floor as she speaks, and all three girls grovel on all-fours on the carpet in search of the missing wedge. By-and-by Diana finds it under the wash-hand-stand, and with it the decrepit window is propped open to admit the gentle April winds.

" I know you are longing for us to go," says Diana brusquely, when this feat is accomplished. " Come along, Bell, come ! it is cruelty to animals to keep her out of bed. Of course we will send our maid to dress your hair in the morning ; she has not at all a bad idea of hair-dressing, though indeed we taught her everything she knows ; she always does ours !"

Joan looks at the colossal heads before her and shudders. "Thank you," she answers, rather hastily, "but indeed I have got quite into the habit of doing my own : I like it ; it makes one feel so independent : good-night !"

Are they really going now ? It seems so. Arabella is already out of the room, and Diana is at the door, when—oh, sorrow !—she returns.

" I hope you do not mind the light in your eyes in the morning," she says, looking up at the window; " unfortunately there is no blind, and the curtains do not draw very well, I am afraid ; there is something the matter with the rings ; but if you pin them over it does nearly as well. Have you got some good big ' corking pins ' ? because, if not, I will run and get you some."

Regardless whether she is speaking truth or fiction, Joan asseverates that she has plenty of corking pins. There is no commodity, however improbable, with which she would not declare herself to be richly provided, in order to obtain the one boon for which her whole sad tired soul craves—solitude.

Gone at last—really gone! And now she may sigh as loudly as she likes, and look round her with as undisguised disapprobation on her surroundings as they naturally inspire. When one is at a very low ebb physically, it takes but a little to overset one. Joan, at her best and strongest—the real Joan— would be ashamed to let any sordid *entourage* make her cry; but she is tired and below par, and tears of forlorn discomfiture fill her eyes, as she looks round on the threadbare carpet—on the large and straggly ugliness of the wall-paper; and notices that a bit is missing from the spout of the ewer.

She stands before the chest of drawers that serves as dressing-table, and looks at herself in the glass that is upon it. "I shall grow like them in time," she says shuddering; "in time I shall learn to talk of men by their surnames, and to have a refreshment-room head of hair!" She pulls her hair down on her forehead to simulate a fringe, sets her hat at the back of her head, and tries to look like them; then, in a paroxysm of disgust, dashes the locks away from her brows and tosses her hat down. "No! I hope I may die first."

She says this aloud, and with such emphasis that her voice drowns the sound of a small knock that comes at the door. It has to be repeated before she hears it; then she hastily pulls her countenance into shape again, and cries, "Come in." (Here they are, back again.)

It is not "they," however. It is only Diana, looking rather shy. You would have said, half an hour ago, that a girl in such a hat and with two such curls could not look shy, but yet she does.

" I have not come for anything particular," she says, speaking very fast and confusedly; " it was only that it struck me just now that we had none of us said that we were glad to see you; we have, none of us, any manners.

I daresay that you have found that out already—but we *are* glad—that is all! I will not come back again."

Whilst making this speech she is redder than any July field poppy, and redder still when, having given Joan a quick and shame-faced kiss, she flies out of the room again, banging the creaky door after her, and leaving Joan remorseful. And Joan's last thought before she closes her fagged eyes in her little hard lumpy bed, which feels as if it were stuffed with good-sized potatoes, is not of her spoutless jug or propped window, of all she has lost and all she is going to suffer— but of the kind and rosy face of her little underbred cousin.

Joan is not very old, but she has already learnt this, that—whether ill-dressed or well-dressed, whether well-bred or ill-bred—love is the one thing very much worth having in this world. If they will love her, she will forgive them everything—even the size of their heads, and their taste for soldiers.

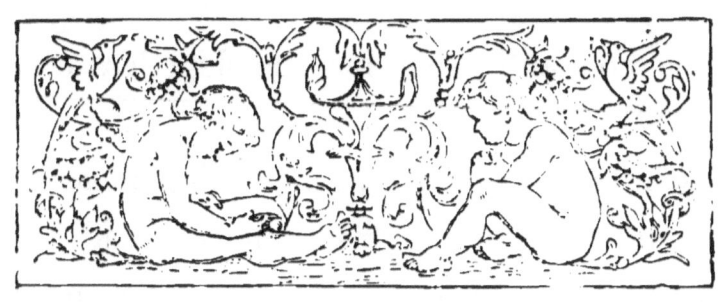

CHAPTER V.

HEN one is twenty years old—
when one's heart is as full of sad-
ness and tiredness as it can well
hold—when one has travelled many hours
at a stretch in a noisy train—then one is
pretty certain to sleep deeply and sweetly,
even though one's mattress be copiously
stuffed with coble stones, even though one's
head be too low and one's feet too high, and
one's bed altogether so surprisingly narrow
as to require very judicious and quiet lying
in, to hinder one from bodily falling out.
Often, in her ocean of down in the green

hung room at Dering, has she slept less completely. Pulses quickly beating to the tune of some past excitement, or coming pleasure, have often made her toss and turn and look eagerly windowwards for the waving of morning's gray flag; but now there is neither excitement behind nor pleasure ahead, and the slower morning comes the better; and so she sleeps.

God is good, and does not even send her a dream. If it came it would surely be a dream of better things and better days, and so it is well away. Not even the unnatural elevation of her feet by the capriciously-stuffed mattress, nor the depression of her head by the little meagre featherless pillow, succeed in giving her a nightmare. She might have been still asleep now had not it been for the inefficiency of the curtain rings, of which Diana overnight had warned her. The corking-pin had indeed drawn the skimped curtains together somewhere about their middle; but up above there is a vacuum through which a wave of morning light rolls and washes under her eyelids. She turns sleepily over on the other side, but even then the wave reaches her, and so does the vigorous melody of a thrush-voice sweetly rebuking her sloth.

> "Good-morrow! good-morrow! the sun was awake
>   Long ago in the blue summer skies;
>   Birds in the brake
>   Carol sweet for your sake.
>   O, lady fair, arise!
>   That morn fresh grace may borrow
>   From your dear eyes."

He says all this so loudly that the sleepy lady has to listen to him. She turns over once or twice again, nearly tumbling out of her strait couch as she does it. But it is useless; both glorious light and happy bird combine to forbid further rest. The bird, indeed, sings another verse:

> "Good-morrow! good-morrow! so whispers the breeze
>   O'er the lake as it flutters and sighs;
>   So murmur the bees
>   From the scented lime-trees.
>   O, lady fair, arise—
>   Arise and give good-morrow!
>   The dearest of replies."

So in despair she sits up, rubs her blue eyes like a child with her knuckles, and looks round. It is a well-known fact that rude and out-spoken daylight tells many home-truths about things that politer candlelight either slurs over or is civilly silent upon. If Joan's new room had looked unhandsome over night by the light of one composite candle, it certainly does not look more lovesome now that day's strong lamp is held up to its shortcomings. It would take a great effort of memory on the part of its owners, a great flight of imagination on the part of Joan, to reconstruct the pattern of the carpet; so utterly has it disappeared under the tread of the numberless feet that have evidently walked upon it. Of paint on door and wainscot there is so little as to be hardly worth naming ; there is a zigzag crack across the looking-glass interfering with one's view of one's nose ; and the piece missing from the water-jug spout is larger than it appeared over night. It is now seen to amount to the

loss of almost the whole spout. But eight
hours of sleep have put new strength and
courage into Joan. Not even the squalor of
having a jug without a spout can make her
cry; she feels as strong and as bright as the
new day. She jumps out of bed, and runs
on bare light feet to the window. She un-
fastens the curtain, carefully laying aside the
friendly corking-pin with a thrifty instinct
born of her new circumstances. Most likely
there is not another in the household. There
is no blind, as you know, to draw up; so at
once she stands face to face with the morning.
It is not early dawn, as she sees at once; it
is dawn's elder brother. The sun is already
pretty high; she looks up at him fondly,
though he rewards her by making the water
pour down her cheeks. He and the moon
are the only two old friends that are left her.
Then she looks out curiously at the prospect.
There is the gate at which her tired fingers
fumbled last night; there is the little mean
sweep up which the execrations of the dogs

accompanied her. Three of them are standing at the present moment watchfully on the
look-out for some passer-by to pounce out on,
and insult. A shabby grass-plot, with a bed
of ill-to-do shrubs, long-legged laurels, and
cypress abortions in the middle; then the
road. A cart full of manure is passing along
it. Bell was right; there is an excellent
view of it. She puts her head farther out to
extend her view. On the right the three
little brother villas. People get up in them
earlier, apparently, than they do here. A
woman is standing at the door of our next-
door neighbour shaking a hearth-rug; beyond
again the great unsightly hospital; larger,
unsightlier than ever by daylight. She shudders. How could any one have built their
dwelling so near that temple of pain and un-
cleanness? She looks away quickly, and turns
her eyes towards the left.

What a contrast! On one hand, disease,
anguish, ugly death. On the other, life that
seems unending; beauty without peer; joy

and mirth unrivalled. A great plain of most
shining silver, laughing in the morning's eyes
—the sea! The sea makes some people
bilious : to other people its immortal restlessness gives the blues. But neither bile
nor blues interfere with Joan's utter love for
it. It is her own familiar friend. She
stretches her arms out towards it, and laughs
aloud in joyful greeting.

After all, there may be pleasant things
yet ahead in life. Whether or not any one
else in the house is up, she, at least, can no
longer waste time in bed. Instinct tells her
that in this establishment it will be useless
to make any efforts towards the obtaining of
hot water. Rather to her surprise, however,
and much to her relief, she finds a great jug
of cold ; a jug with a spout, but (to hinder it
from exalting itself too much above its
brother on this score) without a handle.
Having washed and dressed ; having brushed
her dusty gown with the awkwardness engendered by utter want of practice ; having

plaited her smooth hair and instinctively
tried to make her head look even smaller
than usual—she puts on her hat, opens her
paintless door, and slips quickly and quietly
downstairs. Not a soul to be seen! not a
sound to be heard!

As she reaches the bottom of the stairs, a
great slow-speaking clock from the Hospital
strikes eight. Clearly they do not rise with
the lark at Portland Villa. She goes into
the drawing-room—a tawdry desolation! It
is exactly as it was left over night; furniture
higgledy-piggledy; chair-covers rucked; anti-
macassars awry.

The sun-shafts are smiting, with bright
rebuke, the dead-white ashes in the dreary
fireplace. It is a disagreeable sight, and
Joan hastens away from it. She goes to the
hall-door and tries it : it is locked, and not
all her efforts can turn the key. There is,
however, a door at the back, which is not
only unlocked, but ajar. It has clearly been
open all night.

In the happy consciousness of having nothing worth stealing, the Moberley family is able to throw its portals hospitably wide to any passing burglar. No doubt there was neither lock nor bolt on Diogenes' tub. She walks out into the little garden; a morsel of flower-border first, then a strip of kitchen-garden in all the amiability of unpruned raspberry bushes, ragged apple trees, triumphant groundsel.

Our next-door neighbour has turned his garden into a drying ground : in the morning wind his clothes are flapping and dancing. By a careful survey of them, you may tell approximately the age, sex, and number of his belongings. From these a clean and soapy smell is wafted over the hedge to Joan's nostrils. It does not take her long to make the circuit of the domain. In five minutes she is back in the flower-garden again. It is as if the drawing-room had walked out of doors. There is the same sordid meagre disorder; weedy gravel walks,

long unmown rank grass, an old laurel-tree,
into which, apparently (it having a forked
branch), every odd-come-short that the family
has not known where else to deposit through
a long series of years has been put—a scythe,
several broken pots, a wooden box, a broken-
backed book, a discoloured torn neckerchief,
an old pair of gloves. If Joan look long and
closely enough, no doubt she will discover
among the miscellaneous contents the missing spout of her jug.

The garden has evidently once formed part
of a better, larger one, belonging to an elder
house, which has no doubt been knocked
down to make way for this little smug band
of pretentious bald hovels, for an ancient sun-
dial stands neglected—in its air of out-at-
elbows gentility—on the grass plot. But
amid all the ugliness and squalidness, there
is beauty too. Spring is so generous—April
so open-handed—that they will not pass by
even Portland Villa. They have given it a
pear-tree, all in bridal white; one load of

thick blossom bunches, you could hardly put a pin between them; they have given it also groups of vigorous daffodils, clumps of polyanthus, smelling of spring : milk-white arabis haunted by the drowsy booming bees. Joan smells all the flowers; mounts on the base of the sun-dial; traces with her finger the trite sad sentence on its discoloured face, " Tempus fugit." Tiny lichens, disapproving of the truism, are filling up the letters.

Then she returns to the laurel-tree, and looks carefully and hopefully for the spout of her jug, but it is not there. Still nothing happens : no one is either seen or heard. All the other houses are up and dressed. The scions of Campidoglio Villa are playing in the garden; the wife of Sardanapalus Villa is feeding her chickens; only Portland Villa still slumbers and sleeps. In despair she returns to the house; opens all the doors in succession as loudly as she can; makes her feet tread as noisily as they are able on the oilcloth. It is no use : nobody wakes.

She passes down the little sweep to the gate ; says something polite and suitable to each of the dogs, who all receive her with an extravagant and over-done civility ; passes out into the road with all six at her heels, and saunters towards the sea. Towards, but not to.

Her friend is farther off than she had thought. From her window it had seemed as if, by stretching out her hands, she might with her finger tips have touched the great glancing silver shield. But the nearer she approaches to it, the more its white glory seems to recede. She feels its cool and bracing breath upon her face, but itself she does not reach.

Whether it is the sea air, or the skimped supper over night, or only the healthy working order in which her young organs are, but she suddenly becomes aware of being inexpressibly hungry, and after having walked half a mile or so, turns back in the hope of at length finding the household aroused.

As she reaches the gate again the hospital
clock beats the light air with nine loud delibe-
rate strokes. They must be up by now. Yes,
it is clear that in the interval of her absence
some one has risen, though no one is visible,
for the hall-door is unlocked ; but on peeping
into the dining-room she is dispirited at seeing
no smallest sign of coming breakfast ; only a
depressingly dingy baize table-cloth, and a
general impression of crumbs. She goes out
again into the garden, and tries to recollect
when, at what distant epoch of her life,
she ever felt so hungry before. Oh, if the
daffodils and the polyanthuses were but
eatable !

As she wanders disconsolately about she
hears, after a while, a window thrown up.
Diana, slightly dressed in night attire, looks
sleepily out. Can it be called Diana ? Diana
without any of her distinguishing features :
Diana without her sausage frisettes ; without
her piled false hair ; without the plumed and
flowered abomination of her hat. Diana, as

God made her : not as Helmsley fashions, as
trolloping curls, as cheap loud clothes—as, in
short, the desire to shine in the eyes of the
170th have made her.

It would never have struck Joan as possible
over night that Diana could be a pretty girl.
It comes upon her now with the force of a
surprise that she is one. A little curly head ;
young dewy eyes full of colour and light ;
pinky cheeks ; red lips made for kisses and
laughter. The beauty of a little dairy-maid
indeed, but still beauty. It is difficult to look
vulgar when one is very young, not inordi-
nately fat, and when one has done nothing
disfiguring to oneself. In her night-gown,
with her blowzed hair tumbling into her sleepy
eyes, Diana is not vulgar.

" You out !" she cries in a drowsy voice,
wherein surprise struggles with departing
slumber. " Why on earth did you get up so
early ? is not the day long enough in all conscience ?"

" I never can sleep after eight o'clock,"

answers Joan half apologetically; "and there is no use in staying in bed when one is wide-awake, is there ?"

" I do not know " (indistinctly, with a yawn). " I think it is better than being up, when there is nothing to do."

A pause. Diana leans her arms on the sill, and looks aimlessly out at the wakeful flowers and the preoccupied bees.

" Is your sis—is Arabella up ?" asks Joan, with a small vain hope that one of the household may be up and stirring.

Diana laughs; showing many neat little white teeth.

" Up ! she is not awake !—Bell !" turning towards the inside of the room, and raising her voice, " Joan wants to know are you up yet ? Joan is up and dressed, and out; you must get up ! it is your week for making tea ! if you do not get up I shall come and shake you !"

But not even this threat has any effect. Diana turns again to the window, replaces her arms on the sill, and shaking her head :

> " ' 'Tis the voice of the sluggard ; I heard her complain,
>   You have waked me too soon : let me slumber again,' "

she says, with a laugh ; " she will not be down for a couple of hours."

" Nor you either ?" says Joan, with a sinking heart ; " do you mean to go to bed again too ?"

" I did," answers Diana lazily, twisting one lock of her rough hair round her finger ; " but I will not now, if you had rather that I did not ; have you any idea what time it is ?"

" It must be a quarter past nine."

" Is that all ?" extending her arms, throwing back her head, and opening her mouth in a gigantic stretch and yawn. " I hoped that it was ten, at least ; I always think that there are just twice too many hours in the day, do not you ? unless the band plays, or something is going on up at the Barracks ; but "—with a heavy sigh—" to-day there is nothing—

positively nothing!" Joan is silent. To be
a whole day without soldiers is to her a new
form of suffering, and one for which in all her
pharmacy there is no remedy. " But to be
sure your boxes will come to-day," continues
Diana with a livelier air, rousing herself from
the pensive strain of thought into which she
has fallen; "that will give us something to
do; it will take a long time, no doubt, to
examine all your things."

Joan swallows a sigh, and strangles a
shudder.

" I daresay it will!"

"Maybe they will be here quite early,"
resumes the girl, now thoroughly awakened;
" then I will dress at once : I do not take long
when once I set about it; Bell says twenty
minutes—I say a quarter of an hour; and you
know it does not matter how untidy I am to-
day, as no one will see me."

Joan shudders outright this time, and does
not try to strangle it, as Miss Diana thus
makes herself the naïve exponent of this

doctrine of home slatternliness, and outdoor finery.

" You did not see any sign of breakfast, I suppose," says Diana presently ; happily unconscious of the effect her words have produced ; " nothing laid ?"

" Nothing !"

" I thought not : there never is ; go into the dining-room and ring for breakfast : go on ringing till she comes !"

Joan obeys with alacrity. The hope of food, however distant, gives wings to her feet. The dining-room bell is broken. The rope is lying curled like a shabby snake on the floor. Not liking to take any further measures without directions, she returns to the garden to announce to her cousin her ill success.

She finds her still yawning at the morning sun and the flowers in exceeding dishabille.

" Broken is it ? Oh, so it is ! Billy Jackson did it on Wednesday, when two of them came to luncheon here. Then go to the swing-door and call! go on calling till she answers! she very often pretends not to hear."

Joan does as she is bid, and repairs to the indicated swing-door, where she stands and calls " Sarah!" several times without any apparent result. She hears indeed the sound of voices in colloquy or altercation in some not distant region, but answer comes there none.

The Moberley parlour-maid has evidently laid to heart Swift's "Directions to Servants," and especially this one, " Never come till you have been called three or four times, for none but dogs will come at the first whistle, and when the master calls 'Who's there?' nobody is bound to come, for 'Who's there?' is nobody's name."

But at length, one last despairing cry, hunger prompted, and uttered in a louder key than Joan has ever expected to hear herself employ, evokes a spirit from the kitchen. A pert-faced, black-handed young creature, with a disordered coiffure nearly as big as her mistresses', answers the oft-repeated summons, and having received with a sulky surprise Joan's request for speedy breakfast, mildly yet firmly preferred, retires a good deal more quickly than she came.

CHAPTER VI.

HE family is assembled at length. Di having successfully removed or concealed nearly all traces of the beauty that God has given her. She has, indeed, been unable to do away with her eyes, or make them look as underbred as the rest of her. They still shine and laugh out of her disfigured face. She has, however, violet-powdered her fresh cheeks, piled her hair to more than its pristine height and bulk, and trailed her spurious curls to even greater length than on the previous evening. The dew has apparently taken every

morsel of curl out of them; and as she is
pretty sure to see no one to-day, Diana has
not thought it worth while to re-curl them.

They therefore wander in perfectly straight
and lustreless disorder down her back. Nor
has her sister had less prosperity in the task
of self-disfigurement. Her labour has indeed
been less, as she has had less original beauty
to spoil.

Daylight is no kinder to Mrs. Moberley
than it has already been to her furniture
and her daughters. She looks, if possible,
fatter and hotter than ever; nor do the start-
ing seams of her morning gown, nor the easy
negligence with which her cap sits crookedly
upon her head, greatly enhance the attractiveness of her appearance. It is only a Life-
guardsman to whom it is becoming to have
his cap set on awry.

She has been holding Joan's most reluctant
hand for full five minutes, and staring intently
with a fat pathos into her face, as she tries
to dig out from among her features a resem-

blance to some member alive or dead of her own family. She is interrupted in her hopeless search by Diana, who strikes in brusquely :

" By the by, did the bed fall down with you last night ? I forgot to ask you : it does sometimes; it did once with me. I think its legs are weak ; I was so frightened ; I thought it was the Last Day ; that was why we put it in the spare room !"

" Nonsense, Di !" cries Mrs. Moberley peevishly ; " do not frighten the girl !—perhaps" (turning to Joan) "" it might not bear a very heavy person—I daresay that it would not ; but it will never break down with such a light weight as you."

" I should not think that she was much lighter than I am," says Diana contradictiously, measuring Joan with an appraising eye, " for though of course she is much slighter, she is twice as tall, and it comes to the same thing—hurrah ! there is breakfast at last! I hear Sarah clattering the plates."

Joan is very thankful for any diversion which removes six eyes from her person, and doubly thankful that the diversion should be in the shape of food. A move is made towards the dining-room, which is just across the narrow passage. As she steps over the threshold Bell cries out in a warning voice:

"Take care, Joan! the big hole in the carpet is just there; it very nearly tripped up Micky last Christmas-day."

Joan starts, stumbles, and by catching at the door-post recovers herself.

"If it is of such long standing," she says, with an astonished laugh, "why does not some one mend it?"

"Oh, I do not know," replies the girl indifferently. "I suppose that Sarah has no time; and, after all, it does no great harm when one remembers where it is, and the dogs like it."

Such reasoning is unanswerable, as Joan

feels; and so she takes her seat in silence at the social board. Before she had entered the room, Joan had credited herself with an appetite to which any food short of tripe or haggis would be welcome. She had said to herself reassuringly that they are not likely to have tripe for breakfast. She had pictured herself as pasturing with relish on all manner of plain and homely food, thick bread and scrape, porridge, perhaps treacle. Yes, she would not despise even treacle. But the first glance that she casts on the table arrangements robs her at once of half her appetite—a rumpled table-cloth, rich in yesterday's stains; a dull tea-pot; dim spoons; cups all cracked more or less, mostly more; and not a flower! Not one of all the thousand primroses that are palely smiling from every hedge-row! Treacle! porridge! Who could eat treacle or porridge on such a table-cloth?

Her meditations are interrupted by the sound of the two girls' voices, raised in recriminatory dialogue. They are wrangling as to who shall make the tea, or rather who shall not make it, for it is clearly an unpopular office.

After a few moments of argument of "you-are-another" nature, during which no approach is apparently made to a decision, Joan's soft voice strikes in, or rather steals in, between the shrill sharpness of those of the two combatants:

"If you like I will make tea; I am considered" (with a faint smile) "rather a good tea-maker; I always used to make it at— at—Dering."

As she speaks the breakfast-room at Dering rises before her mind's eye: the breakfast-table in all the loveliness of spotless cleanliness, brilliantly polished old silver, and airy china; the side-board temptingly spread; the wealth of delicate flowers; the kind and courteous old man who always greeted her so lovingly; the pleasant well-bred guests.

Ah! one must not think of these things; one must try to persuade oneself that one has always flourished at Portland Villa, among dirt, pewter, and cracks. Her offer is accepted with effusive gratitude, and she takes her place at the head of the board.

"Take care of the lid of the tea-pot," says Bell, as a parting injunction, "the hinge is broken, so it is loose, and if you are not careful to pour very slowly it tumbles into the cups and upsets them."

"And is it never to be mended either?" asks Joan, with a laugh that tries to be playful but only succeeds in being sad. "Do the dogs like it too?"

Joan's motive for her proposal has been chiefly good-nature, but there has also been in it a grain of self-interest. Behind the urn she will be less observed—less compelled to eat. But here she is mistaken. Diana, whose eyes are apparently as sharp as they are clear and shining, detects the emptiness of her plate and the idleness of her jaws.

"Why, Joan, you are eating nothing!" she cries in a high key of surprise, "positively nothing !—have some beef?" indicating a dish wherein appetisingly repose some thick slices of meat, lavishly daubed with all but raw mustard, and which, apparently, is the nearest approach to a grill that the Moberley *chef* can effect. "No? Some broiled ham then? No? I see—" a flood of colour deepening the rose tints in her fresh face, and a tone of mortification in her voice— "hungry as you are, you can't stand our food;" in a lowered voice, "and I do not wonder."

"Indeed you are mistaken," cries Joan, now thoroughly distressed, reddening till the tears come into her blue eyes, with a vexed scarlet that outflames even her cousin's, and ready to volunteer to eat any abomination that can be offered to her. "If you will let me, I will change my mind. Yes, I will have some—some—beef, please," looking anxiously from one dish to the other to see whose contents she will be most likely to be able to swallow. "Not very much—only a little."

It is on her plate now and they are all looking at her. But the effort is vain. The too plenteous mustard makes her sneeze and cry, the great wedges of coarse meat choke her.

"You cannot manage it?" asks Diana in a disappointed key, after watching the ill-success of her guest's endeavours with an intent interest. "I was afraid that you would not; but" (looking at her with round childish eyes, full of concern and apprehension) "what will you do all the time that you are living with us? It is" (glancing ruefully at the untempting dainties)—"it is never any better than this—you will starve."

"There is not much fear of that!" replies Joan, smiling faintly, though indeed the very same idea has just been presenting itself before her own mind's eye. "But to tell the truth, I do not think that I am quite so hungry as I imagined; at least more bread-and-butter hungry than anything else."

"Give it to the dogs," says Mrs. Moberley

placidly, not disquieting herself much as to any freaks of appetite displayed by her niece. " Here, Mr. Brown, you are the one who do not mind mustard! hi, along!"

Mr. Brown is on the other side of the table, standing on his hind-legs, with his fore-paws on the cloth, but, on hearing himself addressed, drops down on all-fours again, and rushes round the table in a stormy gallop. Too well he knows the manners of his brothers and sisters to give them any chance of interposing between him and his inherit-ance. Joan loves dogs. However noisy, rude, and greedy they may be, she loves them all, and at the present moment she is also deeply grateful to Mr. Brown for reliev-ing her of her beef. So she stoops down and pats his smooth head.

" He is very like a dog belonging to a friend of mine," she says : " by the by, I think he is an acquaintance of yours ; I mean not the dog, but the man. I think—I am almost sure that he said he knew you."

A light pink colours her cheeks as she says these last words—a tint called up by the recollection of the way in which Wolferstan had alluded to his knowledge of her aunt.

" What regiment was he in ?" asks Bell, to whom "man" and "soldier" are synonymous terms. " When was he quartered here ? The 7th were here last, and before them the 35th, and before them the 88th— "

" He never could have been quartered here," replies Joan, " because he is in the Guards, but I believe that he lives near here —at least his people do ; his name is Wolferstan ; do you know any such person ?"

She is looking from one to the other of the three faces round her, and as she mentions the name of Wolferstan a ray of intelligence and recognition illumines them all.

" He said he knew us ?" asks Diana in a tone of surprise and semi-awe ; " he must have meant by sight."

" Nonsense, Di !" cries her mother tartly ; " he does know me quite well. He always takes off his hat to me whenever he meets me in Helmsley!"

"Is not he stylish-looking?" cries Bell enthusiastically; "he looks so nice in church. He looks about him a good deal during the prayers, but he generally goes to sleep in the sermon, and then one can see what a length his eyelashes are!"

"His father was a very *distanggy*-looking man, when first I came here," says Mrs. Moberley pensively, "though no one would believe it now to look at him; he is quite silly, poor old gentleman, and has to go about in a wheeled-chair, with his valet to blow his nose for him!"

"His mother is a made-up old Jezebel!" cries Bell acrimoniously. "Every year her hair is a different colour; she drives past us sometimes in the road, and looks at us as if we were the dirt under her feet."

"And all because she is an Honourable, I suppose," says Mrs. Moberley, shaking her head; "and, after all, it is the lowest thing that you can be in the Peerage, without being nothing at all."

"And so you know young Wolferstan?" says Diana, with an expression of envious interest in her eyes. "Anthony Wolferstan— is not it a lovely name? Do you mean that you know him really—to talk to?"

Joan laughs a little. "Is that so surprising? Yes, I know him rather well; he used to stay at a house in our neighbourhood, and I have often met him in London, and once he spent a week with us last winter, for some theatricals."

"Spent a week with you!" echoes Bell in a voice of astonishment and awe; "then I suppose you must have been quite amongst the county people."

Joan laughs, but most uncomfortably, and involuntarily draws up her white throat.

"I never looked at it in that light before," she says in rather a lower key; "but now I come to think of it—yes, I suppose we were."

"Well, we are not, you know," cries Diana, with a fierce honesty, while a sea of ingenuous scarlet washes her cheeks at the confession. "I need not tell you that : we do not look much like it, do we? We know hardly any one nice except the officers, and perhaps you would not think them nice : I believe that the county people do not take much notice of them; Micky dined at the Abbey—that is the Wolferstans'—once, when first he came, but they have never asked him again."

"He would not go if they did," says Mrs. Moberley, with dignity; "he has said so often and often; he says he never was at such a dull set-out in his life, and that they did not give him half enough to drink."

Diana shakes her head in a manner that expresses her doubts of Mr. Brand's fortitude in rebutting the proffered civilities of the Abbey; but she is wisely silent.

"I am not sorry that Joan is so intimate with young Wolferstan," remarks Joan's aunt, a moment later, "because she will be able to

introduce him to you, girls, at one of the
balls, and, as likely as not, he will give you
each a dance ; they were all at the Dispensary
Ball last year, and I remember thinking
that he looked as if he would like to know
you."

"Then what hindered him ?" says Diana
dryly. " I am sure that we were willing
enough."

" He was too much taken up with that lady
in sulphur colour and sapphires, who came
with their party," says Bell regretfully.

" I never see him that he is not going
on at a great rate with some one or other,
and I always wish that I were the person," says Diana, with a heartfelt sigh ;
" had he a very bad name in your neighbourhood, Joan ?"

Joan's eyes are downdrooped towards her
plate.

" I believe that he was considered a flirt,"
she says, slowly and rather unwillingly.

" What wicked eyes he has !" says Bell,

with zest; "he would be nothing without his eyes."

"We are not badly off for balls in the winter, Joan," strikes in Mrs. Moberley complacently at this point—"not for a country place; there is always the Dispensary, and the Bachelors', and half a dozen private ones, counting carpet and negus things; and then there is always something going on at the Barracks—always!—they, at least, are determined that Helmsley shall not go to sleep if they can help it."

"What should we do without them?" sighs Bell affectionately; "once, Joan, there was a talk of building barracks at Churton, and moving them from here. I do not think that I ever was so miserable in my life, and Diana was nearly as bad; but we should not have stayed here; we should have underlet the house—mother was already talking about it—"

"And *followed* them?" cries Joan, with an irrepressible astonishment and disgust;

"why, you might as well be *vivandières* at once !"

"One might easily be a worse thing !" says Bell pettishly; "but I never said anything about following them; I only said that we should have left this place."

"It is very difficult to do without military society when you have been used to it all your life," says Mrs. Moberley rather pompously; "these children have every right to be fond of the army; their father was a military man !"

"He was an army doctor !" cries Diana, with her apparently ungovernable honesty.

"I never denied that he was a medical man," retorts Mrs. Moberley, with exasperation, "but he was in the army all the same !"

"Nobody thinks anything of the doctors," persists Diana resolutely; "we never do; which of the girls cares to dance with Dr. Slop ?"

"They rank the same as the other officers,

which you know as well.as I do," rejoins Mrs.
Moberley with warmth; "and their uniform
is much handsomer."

"They are not the same thing," reiterates
Diana doggedly, "and whenever I hear you
telling people that papa was a military man,
I always explain, and I always shall explain,
that he was only the doctor!"

CHAPTER VII.

HERE is no reason why an argument of this kind should ever end. Neither disputant ever advances an inch towards an agreement with the other. Nothing will convince Mrs. Moberley that her late husband was not a military man, nor will Diana ever be persuaded that her father was of equal value with his brother officers in the eyes of the young ladies of his day. There is something very heating—not only figuratively, but literally—in an argument. It makes not only the combatants but the onlookers gasp.

Joan feels a physical oppression—a longing
for air—when a lull (caused, not by argument, but by want of breath) having at length
come, the family re-adjourn to the drawing-
room. Two or three trifling improvements
have taken place in the aspect of this apartment since they left it. Most of the dust
has been swept into corners or under chairs.
The dead ashes have left the grate, the pho-
tograph-books and woolly mats on the table
are set at right-angles again, the antimacas-
sars sit smoothly on the chair-backs, but the
spider's banner still waves in airy freedom
from the ceiling, undisturbed by mop or
pope's-head, and the windows—on this love-
liest, sweetest, freshest of April mornings—
are shut. They are French windows, and look
out towards the front to the meagre grass-
plot and the road. Joan stands gazing longingly out through the dim panes at the fairly-
coloured well-scented world outside, turning
over in her mind whether she yet knows her
cousins well enough to ask leave to admit

a little air. Has not her aunt told her that
it is Liberty Hall? Gaining courage from
this recollection, she raises her fingers to the
handle only to discover that there is no handle.
Both of them have gone, apparently, to look
for the jug-spout, the gate-hinge, and the
other missing etceteras of Portland Villa.

"Do you want to open the window?" says
Diana, joining her. "Stay, I will get a pair
of scissors; we always have to open them with
scissors; mother's is the largest pair. The
handles have been gone a long while; but
the fact is, we owe a long bill to the lock-
smith, and we do not like to have him again
till it is paid!"

They are open now, and the morning air,
the noise of the blissful bees, the clean smell
of the arabis float in all together. The dogs
—they are all pugs, more or less—are out on
the turf, employing themselves in different
ways. Mr. Brown is digging violently and
secretly in the corner of the flower-border,
making the brown earth fly up into his own

eyes, and over all his eager face, and Regy
and Algy are rolling over each other in
friendly battle on the sward.   Regy has both
paws round Algy's neck, and Algy has got a
large and baggy piece of Regy's black cheek
in his mouth.   All the clear fine air is full of
thrush voices.   I suppose that every April
the birds say the same thing, but yet it seems
as if each spring their music were bettered,
their little trills more deftly done.   Joan
stands leaning against the door listening to
them, and tapping with one foot on the sill.

" How close you are to the sea," she says
presently, turning her face in the direction of
the great flood, and opening mouth and nostrils to inhale the pungency of thesea wind.
"I suppose that you are down there every
day ?"

Diana shakes her head.

" Not often ; sometimes we go down to
bathe if the tide suits, but not often, it is too
expensive ; what with machine and dresses,
it comes to a shilling every time !"

"And you never walk on the shore?"

"Never," answers Bell, joining in the conversation; "no one does; one never meets any of them—I mean, any one there! If there were a pier and the band played, it would be different; but as it is, there is nothing—absolutely nothing—but sand and cockle-shells."

"Micky sometimes takes his big Newfoundland down for a swim," says Diana, pulling a bit of wallflower and holding it to Mr. Brown's nose, who, having dug his hole as deep as he wished, and disinterred half a dozen innocent bulbs, now makes one of the party. "He throws sticks in for him; it is so pretty to see him riding up and down on the waves, with his great black tail sweeping out behind him, like a feather. Dear old dog! Micky is going to give him to me by-and-by, when he goes away." She says the last four words in a lower softer key, with her head turned aside, and under her ill-fitting pigeon-breasted gown her heart heaves in a sigh.

" *Another* dog ?" says Joan, lifting her eye-brows. " Is he to be indoors or out of doors ?"

" Indoors, of course," answers Diana indignantly. " I should as soon think of turning mother into the yard as of cooping up a dog there; and, after all, one more does not make much difference either way. If one has six, one may just as well have seven."

" We have gone on that principle ever since we had two," says Bell, with a laugh; " we shall get up to twenty in time."

" With all my heart," cries Diana blithely; " for though they do not perhaps improve the furniture, they certainly are the light of the house."

As she speaks she jumps gaily down the steps, and plumping down on the grass-plot, is instantly covered by the six pugs. Three get on her lap, one licks her nose, one mumbles her hand, and two worry the rosette on her shoe.

Joan, laughing, steps out after her; and only the consciousness of her new crape, and the unlikelihood of its ever being replaced, prevent her from joining in the fray.

"Would you like to come out for a walk, Joan?" says Diana presently, lifting her sunshiny eyes to her cousin's face. "I think it would gratify the dogs!—Algy, if you do that once again, I shall pull your tail!—but, perhaps, if you have always been used to your carriage, you cannot walk."

"But I can, indeed," cries Joan eagerly; "nobody better; often and often I have walked round the park at home."

"It will not fatigue you to walk round the park here," says Diana, a little sarcastically, eying her shabby domain; "but if you could condescend to a high-road—"

"We had better take sunshades!" says Bell with alacrity; "there is not much shade, and there is a good deal of dust; but when once you get there the shops are really very good; and the morning is not a bad time either; many of the officers' wives cater for themselves, and one is pretty sure to see somebody !"

"Are we going to the town?" with an accent of unconcealable disappointment, while her thoughts revert to the unlovely tract passed last night—the brick-fields, the scaffolding poles, the Hospital. "Must we?"

There is a little silence.

Diana has bent her head over the dogs.

Bell's jaw has lengthened. "It is the only road where one ever has a chance of seeing any one," she says peevishly.

Diana looks up again. If there was any cloud on her face it is certainly gone again: the blue sky above is not clearer or merrier. "You would like to go to the sea?" she says good-temperedly; "well, we will!—the dogs love a game with the sea-gulls, and they always think that they are going to catch them!"

Ten minutes later they set off. Their party, however, is reduced by one. Bell stays at home. It is one thing to brave the sun shafts and the dust clouds for the cer-

tainty of shops and the hope of officers;
but quite another thing to expose oneself to
these disagreeables merely for the sake of
sand and cockle-shells. But, after all, the
sunbeams shine to stroke, not to smite, and
they come in for but little dust, as their way
lies for the most part across fields—fields
where the future harvest is laughing in
green infancy; where the riotous sap is
racing along the veins of the hedge-row
May-bushes; fields where the meadow grass,
forgetting its wintry pallor, is beginning to
put on again its strength and sweetness.

Joan's soul has gone out of her body—
away from her own tame and meagre lot,
and is frolicking in the spring world, when it
is suddenly recalled by the voice of Diana, in
grave and earnest inquiry:

"Joan, do you like my hat?"

Joan brings back her attention as quickly
as she can from nature to art, and recalls her
eyes from the live lark—the speck of loud
music quivering miles above her head—to

the dead bird of paradise, from whose body
a mighty tail has been reft—a tail that rears
itself aloft and sweeps away behind — to
adorn her cousin's coiffure.

As she does not at once answer (at least
in words), Diana resumes in a rather disappointed voice, but still with confidence : " It
must be all right, for it came from Paris—
Micky brought it me the other day; people
in Helmsley laugh at it a good deal—so I
am told ; but Helmsley fashions are always a
year behind London, and London, they say,
is a year behind Paris ; and so, no doubt, it
will come here in time, and then people will
see that I have been right all along !"

" I was in Paris not long ago," says Joan
slowly, while her eye roves with an expression
of deep distrust over her cousin's head, " but
I do not think that I saw anything very like
it. Are you sure that it came from Paris ?"

" He said so," replies Diana in a crest-
fallen voice ; " and I do not think that he
would tell an untruth about it."

" Of course not!" answers Joan, reflecting that in Paris, no less than in other cities, you may no doubt find abominable head-gears, if you only go to the right places for them.

A little pause.

" You do not like it, then ?" asks Diana diffidently, with a sound of not distant tears in her voice. " I had rather that you would tell the truth."

" I think it is very—very—very—remark-able," answers Joan, distressed and flounder-ing about in search of an adjective which shall be moderately truthful, and not too damnatory. " Has Bell one like it ? Did he give her one too ?"

" O dear, no!" rejoins the other, recover-ing her alacrity of tone ; " he has never given her anything—he is not her friend. Bobby Butler gave her a jacket last winter—a very handsome one—black velvet and sable tails. Bobby paid her a great deal of attention, he always asked her to dance first, and sometimes took her down to supper. Many people thought that he would come out with a proposal some fine day, but he never did; he went away instead!"

Miss Dering makes no audible comment on this piece of news, but to her own heart she says, "Wise Bobby."

"He said very disagreeable things about us after he went," pursues Diana gravely; "laughing at us, you know, and altogether not kind! When we heard it I wanted her to send him the jacket back again. Would not you have sent it back?"

"I should never have taken it in the first instance," answers Joan, drawing up her little head, while her cheeks redden, and her breath quickens. Diana opens her large eyes.

"Would not you?" she says in a surprised tone; "but they were *real* sable-tails, you know—not mock!—well—it was no use! she would not send it back!"

Joan groans a little.

" And what else have they given you ?" she says in a tone out of which she in vain tries to keep the indignant contempt ; " do they dress you altogether ?"

" Do you mean that we ought not to take presents ?" asks Diana, gazing with a little consternation and a good deal of astonishment at her cousin's lifted head and flushed cheeks ; " but, you know, we do not ask for them; they offer them to us, and" (rather faltering) "when one is very badly off, and has very few clothes of one's own, and is fond of being a little smart, it is so hard to refuse !"

Joan is silent ; a silence of anything but acquiescence, as Diana feels.

" I do not want them to give me anything expensive or valuable," she goes on, after a moment or two, in a rather humiliated tone. " I am sure it is the last thing I wish, that Micky should give me a jacket like Bell's, as he sometimes talks of doing ; for I do not think he is well off, and I am sure he could not afford it ; but a hat !—that could not ruin him, I thought, and it was a great matter to me !"

There is such a wistfulness in her tone as she makes this last appeal that Joan feels compelled to smile, but it is the smile of a young Spartan.

" I would sooner have gone without a hat !" she says emphatically ; " or, indeed, without a head !"

They walk on in an uncomfortable silence ; the one irritated and galled, the other crest-fallen and humbled. But before long, the warm shining of the sun, the lark's solo, and the sound of the plash and plunge of the morning waves that they are nearing smooth the creases out of Miss Dering's temper ; and she speaks again : changing, this time, the obnoxious theme, though not getting as far from it as she perhaps imagines.

" What odd names your dogs have ! Algy, Regy, Charlie, Mr. Brown, Willy. They are not like dogs' names !"

" No, they are not !" replies Diana meekly ;

" and indeed they are not dogs' names; we christened them after—after—people !"

" After men you know ?" (lifting her eyebrows again a little).

" After men in different regiments that have been here," says Diana, turning her head half away, and looking foolish ; " men that were— were—friends of ours ! Algy was in the 88th, Regy was in the 35th, Willy was in the 10th, Charlie—I forget what Charlie was in !—it is so long ago ! he is the eldest of the whole lot !"

" And Mr. Brown ?" asks Joan, laughing against her will.

" Oh, Mr. Brown," replies Diana, rather confused ; " well, he used to be Bobby, after Bobby Butler ; but when he behaved so badly to Bell, we thought we would not call him Bobby any more, because it only reminded us ; so we re-christened him after Mr. Brown - who was in the same regiment; he hardly knows his name yet."

" But why *Mr.* Brown ?" inquires Joan,

wondering; "why are you so much
more respectful to him than to the
others?"

"We knew him less," explains Diana
gravely; "we never were intimate with him,
and he never would tell us what his christian
name was—I do not know why—so we had
to call the dog Mr. Brown."

Joan laughs with a sincere though dismal
mirth.

"And when Micky goes, will you christen
another dog after him?" she asks.

"I do not know," replies Diana rather
shortly, turning her head about with an uneasy movement; "he is not gone yet: it will
be time enough to think about that when
he is!"

They have reached the sea; have passed
the loose sand hills, where the dry grass
scantly waves, and the blue sea-thistles blow;
have lightly sprung over half a dozen runlets
racing down to empty their little tea-cups of
fresh sweet water far into the salt and greedy

sea, that takes all presents and says no " thank you " for them.

Now they stand side by side on a stretch of hard sand, on which the foot scarcely leaves a print, and which—were the day sulky and dull—would be called brown, but now are glistening and dazzling with unquestioned gold. Is it not a wealthy day? a silver sea breaking on golden sands, and both arched by a sapphire sky.

The sea is in its civillest humour. With the meekest air, the blandest, sleepiest, most lulling sound, it comes creaming in; deceitfully stealing round their feet as they stand, and coolly fondling them. To-day it is too gentle even to laugh; only it smiles up to the sun, with unnumbered dimples.

> " ' I see the deep's untrampled floor
>   With green and purple sea-weed strown,' "

says Joan, half under her breath, stooping to pick up a length of sea-bloom that, drenched and emerald coloured, has just drifted to her feet; then turning with wondering lips and kindling eyes to Diana :

"And you never come here? you do not like it?"

" I like it well enough," replies Diana apologetically, shading her eyes with her hand from the sun-and-sea dazzle. "Look!" (pointing to a little puff and a small tail of smoke away on the horizon); "there is a steamer! is not it tantalising? they never come any nearer than that: it would be so pleasant if they would come quite close, and one could see who was on board. Yes" (resuming the thread of her discourse), " I like it well enough, as I said; but you see it is not only I; there are two of us, you know, and Bell hates it; she does not care to walk anywhere much except on the Helmsley road, and I must own that one does see six carriages there of a day, for one that one sees anywhere else."

Joan shrugs her shoulders, and flings back her green weed, which, limply clinging round

her fingers, has lost half its native beauty,
into a rippling wave that comes to fetch it,
and on which it floats home again with recovered loveliness.

"It is not quite all Bell's fault either,"
resumes Diana presently, with an uncomfortable sense of having slightly misrepre-
sented things, and laid a heavier burden on
her sister's shoulders than they quite deserve
to bear. "I like the Helmsley road too; I
like going where one is most likely to see
people too; but I do not dislike the sea"
(looking round with a tolerant air on the
august flood before her); "if it were only I,
I should most likely come here a good deal
oftener; and I am rather fond of sea-things.
Once I kept a sea anemone in my wash-hand-
basin for a fortnight, and fed it with raw
beef."

Joan laughs a little at this naïve instance
of love for the wonders of the deep, and then
stoops down pensively to pull the ear of Mr.
Brown, who, either through having more

common sense or being more encumbered
with fat than his brothers, has desisted
earlier from the sea-gull chase, and now sits
on the hard sand, with his heart beating very
fast, and slobbering a good deal as his eyes
follow his late quarry with an expression
which seems to say that the ways of sea-
gulls — luring on an honest dog only to
delude him—are not according to his ideas of
what the manners of a modest bird should
be.

"He *is* like young Wolferstan's dog, now
you mention it," says Diana, stooping too,
and stroking the fine velvet of his other ear;
"and yet they say that he gave five-and-
twenty guineas for his, and we did not give
five-and-twenty pence for you, did we, Mr.
Brown? By the by, Joan" (with quickened
tone and brightened eyes), "we may as well
go home by the Abbey, may not we? as you
know him, you would like to see the place
where he lives, and it is not at all out of our
way."

"If you like," answers Joan in rather a melancholy tone. "Yes, certainly! I suppose that there is no fear of meeting any of them! —that they are all safe away in London?"

"Yes," says Diana, heaving a deep sigh, "safe away in London! lucky people!—as regularly as the spring comes round, off they go! What would they say to me, who have never been to London in my life? Bell was there once, but she did not like it; she said it made her feel so small. I do not think I should mind that—I mean, I am used to it; even here in Helmsley, I never feel **very** large!"

They lapse into silence. The sun has mounted higher. Now that they have left the breeze-beaten shore, and the cool fields, and are tramping along a glaring dusty highroad, he smites on their heads with less kindness and more force. Physical discomfort deepens the gloom of Joan's reflections.

"Have we much farther to go?" she says, after a while, in a rather disconsolate voice, trailing one foot languidly after another in the powdery dust.

"We are just there," answers Diana cheerfully; "there are the gates with their wolf crest on them !—oh, how thirsty I am ! I will ask the lodge woman for a glass of water, and then we can have a chat with her, and she will tell us all about them—when they are coming down."

They have reached the gates; the high and solid stone posts, surmounted by great stone balls, and on each of which a wolf's head with fanged jaws is for ever grinning in stone. The lodge-keeper is apparently out. The lodge-door is shut. Evidently, in the absence of the family, she is taking a holiday from her duties. The hoped-for information about the family is therefore not forthcoming.

"One can get a capital view of the house if one puts one's head far enough through," says Diana, thrusting her hot cheeks between the cool iron bars of the gate, and twisting her neck; "later on in the year, when the scarlet geraniums are in flower, one can see them quite plainly; I fancy they have a lovely garden!"

"Have you never been inside?" asks Joan in surprise.

"Never; it is not a show place, and you know we do not know them; mother says" (in a tone of contempt) "that Colonel Wolferstan knows her, but I do not call it knowing a person to say 'Good-morning, Mrs. Moberley! fine day!' if he happens to meet her; it is my belief that he would not know her even by sight, only that she is so remarkable-looking that it is difficult to forget her when once you have seen her."

CHAPTER VIII.

T is an hour later. They are at home again.

"At what time do you dine?" asks Joan languidly, as a horrible suspicion that a lengthy steaming mid-day dinner is henceforth to be her portion dawns on her mind.

Not even the sight, the sound, the smell, nor the taste of the sea have been able to raise Miss Dering's spirits. Whatever small measure of cheerfulness and buoyancy they inspired have been counteracted by her scanty view through his harshly-closed gates of Wol-

ferstan's home.   It seems to her a grim augury
of the way in which, from this time onwards,
she will make acquaintance with all fair and
pleasant things.   She will peep at them dis-
tantly through iron bars.

"At what hour do we dine?" repeats Diana
reflectively. "Well, to tell you the truth, that
is a fact at which I have never yet arrived :
all I know is, that it is never the same two
days together ; sometimes the butcher does
not bring the meat, sometimes the oven will
not heat, sometimes the kitchen clock stops,
sometimes Sarah forgets to lay the cloth ;
however, it is generally somewhere between
one and three ; though I have known it half-
past twelve, and I have known it four. However, when there is nothing to do all day"
(yawning), "it does not much matter, does
it ? but if you are hungry, as indeed you have
every right to be, let me fetch you a bit of
bread ; I know that there is bread, for I saw
the baker's cart drive away five minutes
ago."

But Joan is not hungry. Not even when, by-and-by, seated at the dinner-table, she watches Mrs. Moberley sawing asunder a gigantic fowl, which has evidently spent a long life in walking; so preternaturally are the muscles of his legs developed : a mammoth bird, flanked by the biggest ham that ever scratched itself in life against a post.

"You might ride to York on this knife!" observes Mrs. Moberley, desisting, heated and baffled, from her efforts, and eying her implement with an exasperated air. "I do not know what has come to the knives of late ; one cannot tell the backs from the blades."

"Micky has spoilt most of our knives cutting soda-water wires with them," says Bell gravely ; "he ought to give us a new set when he goes away, and so I shall tell him."

"Do not!" cries Diana hastily, and reddening; "for Heaven's sake do not let us try to get anything more out of them !"

"Talking of soda-water," says Mrs. Mo-

berley slowly, in the intervals of wrestling
with the mighty pinion before her, "reminds
me that whether you like it or not, girls, into
Helmsley you must go this afternoon; as I
told you last night, we are quite out of soda-
water, and the man has not brought the
beer!"

"I must give my curl a turn with the
irons then," says Diana, pulling out her
long trolloping lock to its full length, and
pensively regarding it; "it was bad enough
this morning, but the sea air has taken out
what little remnant of curl was left in it."

"I have half a mind to go with you
myself, girls," says Mrs. Moberley friskily;
"that is, if you will let me take my time and
not run me off my legs; why should not we
make an afternoon of it—it is a poor heart
that never rejoices—and take Joan round by
the Barracks and the Club Room?"

But against this plan for her entertainment Joan rises in mild but resolute revolt.
Whether she will ever be able to brace her

nerves enough to enable her to let herself be
hawked about among the 170th Regiment has
yet to be decided.   At present she is at some
distance from that consummation.

"Very well, my dear, very well!" replies
her aunt, rather offended; "say no more
about it — say no more — no one in this
house is ever obliged to do anything that is
disagreeable to them : as I told you when
you came, it is Liberty Hall, Joan—Liberty
Hall!"

So she sees them go without her.   It is
some time before they are really off, as—apart
from the matter of the curling irons—an entire
change of costume is apparently necessary.
At length they are ready; the girls with
their cuffs well pulled down over their
knuckles, their dresses freely opened at the
throat, their necks abundantly hung with
lockets, and their hair freshly frizzed—newly
towzled.

"I do not care how many people we meet
now," says Bell exultantly, drawing on a pair

of tight gloves; " the more the better ! Come
along, Di !"

But Diana is apparently not quite so fully
convinced of the unexceptionableness of her
appearance as is her sister. She has glanced
furtively at Joan to see what expression
her eyes wear; and going over to her,
has said brusquely, with uncomfortably red
cheeks:

" I see that you think we have overdone
it—we always do ;" then, not waiting for the
unready answer, " do not be more bored than
you can help while we are away !" she goes
on, moving towards the door, and looking
back rather wistfully from it; " there is a
novel lying about somewhere. I brought it
from the library the other day ; there is a bit
missing from the third volume, but one can
give a good guess what it is about : where
has it gone to, I wonder ?" (glancing round
the room); " I do not see it anywhere—do
you ?"

" Most likely the dogs have got hold of it,"

says Mrs. Moberley placidly.   "Mr. Brown is fond of a book."

"I saw a book in the laurel-tree this morning," suggests Joan doubtfully ; "could that have been it ? it looked rather battered."

"Very likely," rejoins Diana composedly ; "most things in this house find their way sooner or later to the laurel-tree ; well, you will know where to look for it if you want it !"

Now they are gone, not, however, before Bell again puts her head inside the door, to remark in a wheedling voice :

"Even if your boxes come you will not unpack them while we are away, will you ?"

The house door has banged behind them —they have passed down the drive, round the corner, out of sight.   Joan turns from the window with a half-smile on her lips at a last vision of Bell angrily fencing off Mr. Brown from her clean gown with her parasol.   Then she takes out her watch and, with her eyes on its face, makes a calculation.   At Mrs.

Moberley's rate of walking it will take them
quite three-quarters of an hour to reach
Helmsley; three-quarters of an hour to
return. They will surely not spend less than
an hour and a half there : three hours in all.
She has therefore three good hours before
her. Three hours for what ? For reflection ?
In her present situation three minutes would
be too much.

She walks slowly round the room, with her
hands loosely folded behind her. Unspar-
ingly she examines each of the details that
make up so sordid a whole. She discovers
half a dozen latent dust-heaps, a score of
greater and lesser spiders'-webs, a variety of
ink-stains on the table-cloth, and many rents
in the chair-covers.

Then she returns to the window, and drawing up a chair to it, so as to feel all the
honeyed freshness of the air, sits down, and
leaning her sleek head against the faded
woolly antimacassar, thinks. In dreary pano-
rama all the incidents of her short stay, that

yet seems so long, tread past before her
mind's eye.

"I had no idea that I was so greedy," she
says aloud, as her thoughts tarry involuntarily
long at the breakfast which had been so difficult to get through. "Hitherto I have always
thought that I had eaten to live; now I see
that I must have lived to eat!"

She closes her eyes, and past, present, and
future walk solemnly by: the first all sunshiny gold, the second all drab, the third all
ink. Two tears steal out from under her
shut lids, but no sooner does she feel them
on her cheek than she raises herself, and indignantly shakes them away.

"Is this my pluck?" she says, still speaking aloud, though in a low key; "the pluck
of which I boasted even to him? Is this the
way in which I had braced myself to meet
my troubles? just because they are not of the
kind I expected, are they to find me limp
and puling like this? Just because I expected a stab, and have found pin-pricks

instead. Oh! I had rather have been
stabbed—stabbed deep! Any stab would
have been better—anything would have been
better!" she says, twisting her hands together
and writhing at the thought of the daily,
hourly, momently penance to which every
tone of voice, every movement, every mode
of thought of the Moberley family condemns
and will for ever condemn her. " Well,"
rising again, and again beginning to walk
about the room, " well! I suppose that no
one can pick and choose their afflictions. If
I had had my choice, I should have lived with
gentlefolks, and they should have bullied me,
they should have had next to no hair on their
heads, and should never have mentioned a
soldier." She laughs a little, and then, lapsing into deeper gravity, says presently, " God
give me pluck to keep up a good heart and
bear my pin-pricks."

It is a real prayer, though, perhaps, not
conventionally worded. Occupation of some
kind she must have; but what? Her boxes

not having yet arrived, none of her own re-
sources are within reach. She looks rather
hopelessly round the room—not to criticise
this time, but to search. The sight of a
work-basket disgorging tangled Berlin wools
puts an idea into her head. Why not mend
the hole in the dining-room carpet?

Joan has been taught stitching in all its
branches, and, what is more, she loves it.
She has never before, indeed, been set to
mend carpets, but she has mended rents in
other things, and, after all, it is only the ap-
plication to a new purpose of old knowledge.
In three minutes, armed with a darning-
needle and a skein of wool, with her gown
turned inside out and pinned round her, she
is kneeling on the dusty carpet, her whole
soul absorbed in the endeavour to make the
ragged straggly edges of the great rent approach each other.

There is something very soothing in work,
especially handiwork. As Joan toils the
blood runs to her head it is true, but the

bitterness goes out of her heart. A sense of amusement takes its place.

What if that very fine lady, her late maid, could see her now ? What if any of her former friends ? What if Wolferstan, arriving unexpectedly from London and coming to pay his promised visit, were to peep in through the window and see her? She looks up involuntarily, half expecting to meet his eyes smiling in upon her. But no ! Through the casement—the wind has risen a little—she sees a blue and yellow tom-tit swinging to and fro, in airy jollity, on the topmost twig of the little sere cypress outside—that is all. So she resumes her task. After a while she straightens herself, and, sitting up again, speaks out loud :

" There is nothing more revolting than ingratitude," she says emphatically ; "they were ready to give me their very best—it is not their fault that their best is so exceedingly bad. They were willing even to go shares with me in Micky." She laughs softly with a genuine mirth. "Well! I have no Micky to halve it is true, but I can make as great a sacrifice; I will let them copy all my best gowns in red and yellow calico!"

Again she laughs; and so falls to work again. The yawning gap has already disappeared, and is replaced by a lattice-work. To and fro, along and across, quick and sure, the darning-needle goes.

There is still another hour's work before her. As she so thinks, the door-bell, ringing, clangs upon her ear. It cannot be that her cousins are returned already. It must be some one come to call.

"One of *them* perhaps!" she says a little sarcastically; "who knows? — Micky himself? What a bitter disappointment it will be when they come back and learn what they have lost!"

After a pause, and two more applications to the bell on the part of the visitor, Sarah is heard going to obey the summons. The door opens; there is a parley; it closes again.

Sarah returns along the passage. What a heavy foot she has! How ponderously she treads.

Secure in the consciousness of not having a single acquaintance in Helmsley; sure of having neither part nor lot in the visitor, and confident, therefore, of remaining undisturbed, Joan has not taken the trouble to change her position, or lift her head. She is still kneeling, still darning, when a loud and palpably artificial " H'm !" uttered in an unmistakably masculine voice, makes her start violently and look hastily up. Even if Sarah could simulate a manly tread, it would be impossible for her or any other known parlourmaid to counterfeit such a voice.

A perfectly unknown man stands before her—a young man, and, judging by his appearance, an extremely healthy one : a young man, holding a hat in one hand and a stick in the other, and with a confident smile of extreme friendliness both on his lips and in his gay bold eyes.

"Mrs. Moberley is out," says Joan, rising quickly, but without hurry or discomfiture, from her lowly posture, and bending her head slightly in polite but grave salutation.

"And are the girls out too?" asks the young man in a voice that fitly matches in depth and gruffness the sound of his introductory "H'm!" and preparing to deposit his hat and stick in the hall, with an evident intention of staying some time.

"My cousins are out!" answers Joan, with a slight but intentional accent on the two first words, and infusing a little more ice than before into her tone. "I suppose that Sarah must have misled you by the idea that they were at home?"

"No, she did not," replies the young man nonchalantly; "she told me that they were out—that no one but you was at home; but I thought that—" He is looking full at her as he speaks—at the soft yet proud seriousness of her face—and something in it (he himself could not have told you what) makes him change the end of his sentence. He had meant to say, " I thought that I would come in and have a chat with you." He says instead, " I thought that I would come in and wait till their return ! You know " (with a half-awkward, half-familiar laugh) " I am quite a tame cat here—in and out whenever I like."

" Yes ?" in a rather more frozen key than before.

How tall she is ! He had no idea, as she knelt, how tall she was. Both her cousins, both the Moberleys and he, had agreed that she would be a little woman—one can grow much more quickly intimate with a little woman. There is something rather confusing, even to a person who does not know what shyness is, in having a tall young vestal standing opposite to him, looking calmly at him with a grave and, as he feels, not admiring composure, and evidently expecting him to go. It is clear that she can have no idea who he is.

"As there is no one here to introduce us to each other," he says, with a rather nervous laugh, "I suppose we must introduce ourselves. I have no doubt that we have heard each other's name very often."

"I have not yet the pleasure of knowing what your name is," answers Joan gravely.

She has unpinned her gown, and it now hangs in heavy simple folds around her. She is still looking at him.

He wishes that she would look away. He laughs again more nervously, and also louder.

"If you have heard it half as often as I have heard yours, you have every right to be sick of it."

This remark does not seem to Miss Dering to require an answer, so she makes none.

"My name is Brand," he goes on, speaking fast and uneasily, while the naturally healthy tint of his cheeks perceptibly deepens. "I think you must have heard them mention it. I am here most afternoons. I see a great deal of them."

" Yes."

A little silence. The tom-tit still swings and sways on his cypress twig; the rooks are sailing home towards the Abbey, Wolferstan's rooks sailing homewards through the placid sea of air; the shadows are beginning to grow.

" Do you expect them back soon?" says Mr. Brand presently, shifting restlessly from one foot to the other, and growing ever more and more uneasy under the cold shining of his companion's eyes. " Did they say, when they set off, how long they meant to be away?"

" Most of the afternoon, I think."

" And left you here all alone?"

" I preferred it."

" At all events they have lost no time in setting you to work," he says, with a brusque laugh, glancing at her late occupation, and trying, by a great effort, to resume his gaiety and assurance.

To this observation Miss Dering vouchsafes no reply of any sort.

Another pause.

A lamb in the meadow over the road—a lamb that has evidently mislaid its mother—bleats in loud complaint.

"If you really think it worth while to wait for their return," says Joan presently, with a rather severe intonation, "perhaps you will come into the drawing-room." As she speaks she leads the way across the narrow passage, and ushers in her unwelcome visitor. "I fear that you will find it tedious," she says formally, "as I do not expect them back till six or seven. If you will excuse me, I will return to my work."

So saying, and again bowing slightly, she walks out of the room and shuts the door after her. Then repinning her gown, she kneels down again, and re-settles to her toil. An amused smile passes over her features that have lately been set in so austere a gravity.

"So this is Micky," she says to herself.

" Well, like everything else, he is rather worse than I expected."

For some time absolute silence reigns. No sound whatever issues from the drawing-room. After a while, however, there is a noise as of some one walking about to and fro, up and down, in the confined space. Apparently time is beginning to hang on Mr. Brand's hands. Then the piano is opened, and sounds arise from it. It is very much out of tune ; several of the upper notes are quite dumb, and Micky is but a poor performer. Apparently he is trying to pick out the " Dead March " in *Saul* with one finger on it. Thence he slides rather suddenly into " Take back the heart that thou gavest," which he accompanies with his voice. Then he leaves off altogether. A few moments later he opens the door.

" Would you mind my leaving this open a little ?" he asks in a voice a good deal less confident and more respectful than that which he had at first employed ; " it need not dis-

turb you, and we might have a little conversation."

"Certainly, if you wish."

Having gained the permission, he leans
against the doorpost, with his legs crossed,
and his hands in his pockets, but at first the
little conversation does not seem forthcoming.
At length, "It is wonderfully warm weather
for the time of year," he says. He has
evidently been searching among his repertoire
of remarks for one warranted not to give offence, and has been unable to find anything
less obvious than this.

"Yes."

"It is too good to last, I fear; we shall
have the east wind back to-morrow, probably."

"Probably."

"Was there a good deal of east wind at
your—where you came from?"

"A good deal."

A pause. Joan is aware that Mr. Brand's
eyes are fastened immovably upon her; but as
he can see nothing but her tightly-coiled hair

and the nape of her neck, she is not much concerned.

"If you will excuse my asking," in a rather diffident voice, "are you really first cousin to the Misses Moberley? I think I must have misunderstood, but I thought they said *first*."

"Yes, first."

"First cousins are such near relations," pursues the young man, "next thing to being sisters."

"Not quite that," rejoins Joan quickly, involuntarily raising herself, and looking up.

"But next step to it," repeats the other persistently. "I suppose that your mother and Mrs. Moberley were sisters?"

"I suppose so," echoes Joan dreamily, still sitting up, forgetting her work and Micky, and staring blankly before her, while the monstrousness of this proposition strikes her with fresh force and novelty; "I mean—yes—of course they were!"

"You take after your father's family, I suppose?"

"I suppose so," rather shortly, with a thought that the conversation is growing undesirably personal, and resuming her needle.

Another silence; as far as Miss Dering is concerned, it may last for ever; there is nothing embarrassing in an occupied silence, but to be totally idle, and as totally dumb, is confusing.

So Micky feels apparently, for he begins again: "Had you a long journey yesterday?"

"Rather long."

"Railway travelling is very fatiguing, is not it?"

"Very."

"Not so bad as one of the old coaches, though, I daresay?"

"I daresay not."

"Particularly if you went inside?"

"Yes."

Again the lamb, the rooks, and the tom-tit have all the talk to themselves. But Mr. Brand is not easily either baffled or silenced. After a few moments he begins again.

"The gi— I mean your cousins, are very good walkers."

"Are they?"

"Are you a good walker?"

"Pretty good."

"It is a—a—very healthy exercise."

"Yes."

"Not so healthy as riding, though, doctors tell you."

"No."

"Walking is fatigue without exercise, and riding is exercise without fatigue, they say, do not they?"

"I believe so."

"Your boxes are come!" cries a voice, loud and shrill with excitement, breaking in at this point, as Bell's face, hot with running, and reddened by pleasurable agitation, looks in like a very full-blown rose at the window—

"at least they will be in two minutes; we passed the carrier's cart. I ran on to tell you; they quite fill it. Diana says she counted seven; what can you have in *seven* boxes?" She stops out of breath; then, catching sight of Mr. Brand, "Well, it never rains but it pours! you here!"

"I am here so very seldom that that is a most astonishing fact, is not it?" answers the young man, coolly advancing, with a languid air of completest easiest intimacy, to meet his young friend.

Bell is in the house by now, and, having pulled off her hat, is fanning her heated cheeks with it. "Why, you told us that you were to be on guard all to-day!" she says reproachfully.

"But you see I am not!"

At the utter and almost contemptuous familiarity of his tone, Joan looks up in angry astonishment. Can this be the young man who, for the last half-hour, has been laboriously dragging up respectable truisms from

the depths of his being, and diffidently presenting them to her?

But there is no anger on Bell's face, only a
gratified mirth. "So you two have been
making friends, I suppose!" she goes on
gaily; "it is rather late in the day to introduce you to each other, is not it? have you
been making friends?"

As she speaks she looks, smiling inquisi-
tively, from one to the other. A little pause.

"Query? have we?" says the young man at
length, with a laugh happily compounded of
swagger and embarrassment.

But Joan affects to be deaf to the question,
if it is one. She has walked to the window,
and is looking out.

"Seven boxes," resumes Bell, returning
to the subject which is uppermost in her
thoughts; "what can you have in seven
boxes? It will take us quite a whole day to
go through them, will not it?"

"Quite!" replies Joan, sighing.

⁎　✦　⁎　⁎　⁎

It is evening now. Mr. Brand has at length gone, and the candles are lit. "I never was so sure as you were, mother, that they would get on well," Bell is saying, apropos of her cousin and Micky, as she watches the latter's retreating figure lessening down the star-lit road, and shaking her head. " Micky hates being on his P's and Q's ; he likes girls with whom he can be quite at home, at once—who do not mind what he says to them ; that is why he likes us so much, often and often he has said so !"

" A left-handed compliment is not it ?" says Diana, with a rather bitter laugh. " It strikes me that most of our compliments are left-handed ones !"

CHAPTER IX.

HUS Joan has over-lived one day of her new life. She has even begun upon another, for it is morning again. If she has over-lived one, she can over-live all. Probably one will be no better or worse than another. It is possible indeed that use may bring some slight alleviation to her sufferings. Use may adapt her palate to the Moberley dishes; may harden her eye to the Moberley stains and rents. Use may accustom her ear to the staccato music of the Moberley voices, and train her mind to find food and occupation in the Helmsley Barracks.

As long as each day comes singly, each freighted only with its own load, people can bear a great deal.

Thus Joan thinks, as she strolls after breakfast among the lanky gooseberry bushes, with all the dogs at her heels or trotting companionably before her, and with the children of Campidoglio Villa peeping at her through the ragged quickset hedge. After half an hour, spent in trying to cudgel her spirits into content and cheerfulness, she strolls back again to the house; and a quarter of an hour later is walking thoughtfully under an umbrella, and with her hands full of wall-flowers, to the sea. To-day, no one has offered to accompany her. Bell's opinion of the ocean she already knows, nor is Diana so much addicted to the wonders of the deep as to wish to visit them twice running. So she is alone—alone but for the dogs; the dogs that can rub no one the wrong way; who have no preference for soldiers over civilians, wear no false tails, and try to mitigate the blackness of their faces by no pearl powder or cream of roses.

Mr. Brown is carrying a long stick—so long that it nearly trips him up, as he gallops bravely past, defiantly eying the other dogs out of the corner of his eye. She stops to look at three cart-horses drinking at a muddy pool, with collars down, slipped over their necks. She wonders how they drink. They do not seem to open their mouths at all; rather to inhale the water through their nostrils. Already she feels soothed. Every trouble is easier to bear out of doors than in-doors; and this is true, not only of a great grief but of a small vexation. The birds of the air, the beasts of the field—yes, the gawky lambs and solemn flapping rooks, the very winds and flowers help to carry one's load for one. By the time she has reached the sea, she can think with toleration even of Bell and her fur coat.

She is beside the great water now, and with a long sigh of content, sits down on the

shingle. Having explained to the dogs
kindly but firmly that she does not wish for
sandy paws round her neck, or for hot red
tongues licking her cheeks; having begged
Mr. Brown to cease goggling at her so affectionately, and directed his attention to the
insolence of the sea-gulls, she remains at
peace, with her hands clasping her knees and
her looks directed to the loud glad flood. She
watches the large brown waves turn over,
lengthily curling, with a booming noise, in
the sun; tossing high their foamy heads in
the wind, running up to lay their myriad
snow-white foam bubbles at her feet, and
then drawing back again with a sucking
sound, carrying with them the wet
pebbles.

A sea bird of some kind—a diver of engaging manners—is serenely riding up and
down, up and down on the wavering heaving
plain; plunging every two minutes, with a
little splash, into the green depths, and coming
up again black-headed and complacent, a

hundred yards from the spot where he disappeared.

She does not know how long she sits watching the sea's courtship of the land—the obstacles that its patience overcomes. There is a ridge of sand between her and the rising tide; it is with trouble, with many intervening discouragements, with repeated efforts, that it climbs the sandy rise, and then joyfully and swiftly pours over its yeasty streams. Why does not the wave break all at once? Instead of doing so, it curls over in one place; and then the curl runs along the line, until the whole proud breaker is dissolved into quick and hissing froth. Ah! this one has come farther than any of his predecessors— he is sucking in amongst the small stones at her very feet.

> " The lightning of the noontide ocean
>   Is flashing round me, and a tone
> Arises from its measured motion,
>   How sweet did any heart now share in my emotion !"

She says this aloud, after a way that she

has ; but her voice is so soft and the sea is so loud that no one, even if close to her, could hear the words. No sooner are they out of her mouth than she catches the sound of a footstep on the shingle behind her—a quick firm step. What if it be Micky? What if her poetic aspiration after companionship be all too soon answered? What if Micky be come to

"Share in her emotion?"

He is quite capable of it. She looks round in hasty fear, her features already beginning to dress themselves in the austerity with which yesterday she had chilled that brave man's too easy greeting ; but there are other men in the world beside Micky Brand, and this is one of them. Not even in the most ill-lighted room, the dimmest evening light, could you mistake him for Mr. Brand, and, indeed, he would be very much disgusted with you if you did. It is Wolferstan. In a moment the austerity has fled ;

dispersed and routed by a surprised red smile.

> " ' 'Twas when the seas were roaring
> With hollow blasts of wind,
> A damsel lay deploring
> All on a rock reclined !' "

he says, with a low laugh, that mixes pleasantly with the noise of the tumbling waves, as he gently and gaily takes her ready hand.

" But I am not ' on a rock,' and I am not ' deploring ' ;" answers the girl, laughing too.

" She told me that you had gone to Helmsley," he goes on presently, still prisoning in his her small cool fingers, and looking at her with an intentness of scrutiny by no means inferior to Mr. Brand's yesterday one (but which yet does not provoke in her at all the same chastely irate emotion) in his happy handsome eyes ; " but I took the liberty of disbelieving her ; I knew you had not !"

" Who told you that I had ?"

" The servant at your—at Mrs. Moberley's. I have been to pay you a visit."

"And did you see any of them? My aunt—my cousins, I mean?" asks Joan quickly and nervously, while the red hurries up to her cheeks.

The smile on his face broadens, and his eyes light up mirthfully.

" I saw them, and I did not see them; I think they saw me; I think they were reconnoitring me from behind the blinds." A moment later, still speaking playfully, but with a caressing tone in his low voice: "I knew you had not; I knew that I should find you here. After all, you see, though they are your relations and I am not, I know your ways better than they do."

A little pause, filled up by the wash of the morning waves, while the two young people are looking eagerly, and, as it were, half wonderingly, at each other. Though the space of time since they last met is so short, each seems altered in the other's eyes.

Joan is wondering that it had never before struck her what a sweet-toned voice he has;

what a fine and polished enunciation; what
race-horse nostrils! Can it be possible that
in her former life all the men had sweet full
voices, polished enunciations, fine-cut nostrils? and is it the contrast to her present
surroundings—to the Moberley voices, accents, noses—that makes Wolferstan's ex-
cellences start out with such new saliency?
Perhaps it is the lovely setting of the picture :
the sea, the sky, the tawny sands that make
it seem so goodly. One cannot gaze dumbly
for more than five minutes at a time at the
handsomest live picture without growing embarrassed, and so Joan finds.

" And you?" she says presently, breaking
shyly and hastily the happy silence; " what
has brought you here?"

" Do you mean to say that you do not
know?" (in a voice of low reproach). His
eyes are still meeting hers; it seems as if
they would not let them go.

She shakes her head.

" You cannot even guess?"

" No."

" You can lay your hand upon your heart and tell me so ?"

It is a good opportunity for loosing her hand from its long bondage, so she does as he suggests, and laying her hand on that spot in her black dress, under which she feels the regular healthy pulsing of her young heart, says :

" I cannot guess."

" On your word ?"

" On my word."

" On your honour ?"

" Do you wish," says Joan, smiling gravely, " to make me say that I think it was to see me that you have come down ?   Is that what you are trying to drive me to ?"

" That is what I am trying to drive you to."

It is now her turn to look reproachful, and with her the emotion is perhaps more genuine than it was with him.

" How much the better would you be," she says, looking up at him with the limpid sincerity of her eyes, "if you did succeed in making me say what you know as well as I do not to be true? I think I have forgotten how to bandy pretty speeches; life has grown so matter-of-fact that I take everything *au pied de la lettre.*"

"Is it a pretty speech?" he says, with an air of injured innocence which, if counterfeit, is certainly very ably done. "Unless you had suggested the idea, it would never have occurred to me that it was one; and, after all, why should not a pretty speech be occasionally as true as an ugly one? Far be it from me to say that they are all true, or even" —laughing—"that all mine are, God forbid! but this one—" He stops expressively.

She shakes her head disbelievingly, and turning from him, sits gravely down again on the shingle.

"What other motive could have brought me?" he asks eagerly, stretching himself on the sand beside her. "Do you think that it can be very amusing sitting down to dinner in a totally empty house, with no society but brown-holland-swaddled chairs and bagged chandeliers? with an elementary kitchen-maid to cook your dinner, and a charwoman to bring it you, do you?" waiting resolutely for an answer, but he gets none.

Joan's eyes are fixed on the broad band of wondrous purple that stretches in royal beauty across the mid-ocean, at the ineffable greens and blues, like the colours of a pea-cock's neck, with which the waves are shot through and through.

" If you would be so good as to look at me," he goes on presently, with a tone of slight irritation, noting the direction of her eyes, which is not such as he either wishes or intends ; " you would see that for once in my life I am speaking truth ; well !" (after wait-ing a moment in vain) " well ! as you will not, I must trust to the veracity of my voice ; as sure as—" (looking vaguely round for something to adjure) " I do not think that I see anything particularly sure anywhere about,

so I will use no asseveration—I came down ;
I made a disagreeable journey at an incon-
venient time ; I ran the risk of damp beds,
and the certainty of bad dinners, wholly and
solely to see whether you were yet alive !"
(a moment after, in a softened voice) " you
know that transplantation kills some
plants ; how could I tell that you were not
one ?"

Joan laughs a little. " It would take a
good deal more than that to kill me," she
says ; " I am sure that I should be as hard
to kill as an eel. I believe that if I were
cut in two, each half of me would walk away
unhurt, as they say is the case with some
insects."

" And you have over-lived it ?" he says
slowly, with a genuine wonder in voice and
eyes, as his thoughts revert to the peep he
has lately taken at the Moberley establishment, over the grimy parlour-maid's shoulder,
and behind the Moberley blinds.

" It seems so."

" And you are—are—are getting on pretty well ?"

The question sounds inanely bald, and so it seems to himself; but from the nature of the subject it is difficult to make it more precise.

" Getting on !" repeats Joan reflectively, with her blue eyes pensively fixed on a far red sail; " I am alive, as you say, and I am in very good health, and I am not beaten or starved; on the contrary, I am very kindly used; if that is to be ' getting on '—yes—I am getting on nicely !"

" And—and there is no change ?" pursues the young man, embarrassed, but eager; " nothing — nothing pleasant has happened since we last talked ?"

She moves her eyes slowly from the distant brig, and fixes them with a half ironical smile on his face.

" Do you mean have I yet woke to find myself wealthy ? has any one left me a fortune ? well, no ! not yet ! I am still luxuriating on my godfather's thousand

pounds." A moment after, the smile on her
face spreading, and growing into a soft laugh
of genuine amusement : "I now know why
you were so anxious that I should see Mrs.
Moberley—no—do not look miserable! I
will promise not to tell her; and even if I
did, she would not bear malice; she is far too
good-natured! I have also ascertained the
extent of the park; the number of whose
acres I was so determined to learn from
you."

"Do not!" cries the young man hastily;
looking thoroughly foolish; growing extremely red; and galloping off *ventre à terre*
into a different subject. "No other will has
been found then ?"

"None, except the old one, made before I
was born : I knew that there would not be :
he meant to have added a codicil to it; the
lawyer was to have come down on the very
day !—twenty-four hours made a good deal
of difference to my future, did not they ?"

She sighs profoundly, and again turning to

the sea, fixes her eyes dejected and patient on the broad flood.

"How could he leave such a thing till the last moment?" cries the young man, with wondering anger; "what culpable — what inexcusable negligence!"

She brings her eyes quickly back again to his face, but they are meek no longer; instead, flaming and flashing. "Do you think it can make things much easier or pleasanter for me to bear," she says indignantly, "to hear him abused? when you say such things you make me regret that I have ever broached the subject to you; how could he tell that it was the last moment? he was only seventy-two! people oftener than not live till eighty or ninety nowadays: he seemed no more likely to die than you do; does any one ever think that he himself will die? he knows that every one else will, but he does not believe that he will!" After a moment, in a softer gentler voice of deepest emotion: "My one prayer and trust is," she says, "that he does not know — that he cannot see! oh! God could not let him see! it would be too cruel! it would break his heart! he that never thought anything could be good enough for me!"

Her voice wavers and breaks. The tears crowd up into her eyes. A rather prolonged silence. Joan's wet eyes go back to the sea, and absently watch the breakers, idly puzzled to see that a big wave with an imposing volume of brown water and noise of foamy froth sometimes does not reach as far as a lesser humbler one that follows. It is she that at length resumes the conversation. Wolferstan, in fact, is feeling snubbed; and though not exactly bearing malice, has no intention of laying himself open to a second rebuke.

"Apart from any question of *will*," she says thoughtfully, "I wonder how I manage to be left so destitute; at the time I was too miserable to think or reason about it, but since then it has often puzzled me: my father must surely have had a younger son's portion, and as I was his only child, it would naturally come to me, would not it? I know nothing of law, but it seems to me that it must be so."

She looks appealingly at him for confirmation or contradiction; but where are Wolferstan's manners? Is he sulky or only inattentive? He has turned quite away from her, and makes no answer good or bad to her appeal. She is too pre-occupied much to heed his lapse from civility, and goes on:

"Of course I can quite understand, now, why he never mentioned my mother's family to me. I suppose there never was any one who knew less about their parents than I do: I do not even know when and where they first met—when they were married—how long they lived together—"

She stops abruptly, becoming suddenly aware of her auditor's want of attention. His face is still quite turned away, and he has uttered no sound, good or bad.

" You are bored by these details ?" she says a moment later, after a rather hurt silence ; " and no wonder indeed ! I beg your pardon, but" (with a rather desolate smile) "here I am so poor in friends that, like the Ancient Mariner, I button-hole any stranger I chance to meet."

She rises to her feet as she speaks, and prepares to set off homewards. He must look round now—must utter. And he does. He also rises, and turns towards her the face that for the last five minutes he has been so carefully averting. It is redder than its wont. His countenance is troubled, and in his eyes is an expression she does not understand. But even now he makes no reference to the subject of her remarks. He only says in a constrained voice :

" If you think I am bored you are mistaken." Then, a moment after : " Are you going home already? Must you ?"

" Unless I wish to lose my dinner," she answers, with a smile :

" Your luncheon, I suppose you mean ?"

" I mean my dinner; we dine at two—at least we oscillate between that and four."

" Good heavens !—and is that all ? Have you nothing else—nothing more to look forward to the whole of the livelong day ?"

" We have tea and muffins at eight—at least between that and ten."

" Good heavens!" (throwing back his handsome head and looking up in shocked appeal to the turquoise sky).

" And brandy and soda-water all day long, if we like it."

" Good heavens !"

" I have hit the right chord now, have not I ?" says Joan, with a smile of soft malice ; " this is the one of my misfortunes that really touches you. You were bored before " (with gentle persistence), "though you will not own it; but now you are all interest and alert compassion. I have found the right way to your heart—to every man's heart!"

They are walking slowly homewards, side by side, over the thin and bitter grass of the sand-hills, and back into the pleasant meads by which Joan had come.

" You know you must not proportion your pity for me to what your own sufferings would be under a two o'clock dinner," says Joan presently, with a humorous smile.

" They would be severe, I own," he answers gravely. " I know no one, the pleasure of whose society would outweigh them; you, somehow, have a knack of making me speak the truth against my will, and I will own to you that I do not think I should enjoy dining at two o'clock, even with you."

She laughs a little; and again they walk on over half a field in silence.

" I hope," says Joan by-and-by, " that you will not go away with the impression that I am a great object of compassion. I feel as if I had been giving you that idea, and in-

deed it is not the true one. No one can
expect to go through all their lives quite
smoothly; and perhaps those are best off who
have their troubles while they are young—
one is so strong when one is young; probably
I shall have a prosperous middle age, or a
serene old age, or a very easy death to make
up to me—depend upon it, it will be made up
to me in some way."

" By a serene old age," cries Wolferstan
contemptuously. "God forbid! No!—take
my word for it" (looking down with a more
unveiled admiration than he has yet allowed
himself in the eyes, whose wickedness Bell
Moberley commends, at the profile beside
him—the little sensitive fine nose—the sweet
white cheek, clear and clean as privet flowers
—the curled cherry lips), "there is something better than that ahead of you. There
is plenty of fun in life for such as you, between now and your serene old age" (with a
mocking accent).

" Is there?" says Joan a little doubtfully.

"I should not be sorry to think that there were; but if not I can do without it—I can do without it." After a pause: "It is impossible," she says in a more cheerful tone, "to be quite unhappy as long as one is thoroughly healthy, as long as one is honestly trying to do one's best, and as long as one has a keen sense of the ridiculous. This world's beauty," looking fondly at all the brave show of young greenery round her—"this world's beauty is a great boon, but I think that its little ridiculousnesses are a still greater! There are very few things or situations in which I do not find something to make me laugh."

They have come to the end of the fields, have crossed the stile that leads back into the road. To arrive at Portland Villa you must turn to the right, to reach Wolferstan's home to the left.

"We will say good-bye here," says Joan gently but resolutely, holding out her hand. "If you escorted me to the house Mrs. Moberley would invite you to luncheon, and you would find it difficult to evade her importunities."

" Why should I evade them ?" asks Wolfer-stan, to whom the problem of how he is to pass the afternoon has been, for the last half-hour, growing ever more and more insoluble, and who has now grasped the desperate resolution of braving the Moberley food (indubitably very awful, if it all tallies with the appearance of the parlour-maid), yet sweetened by Joan's smiles, and lit by the warm blue fire of Joan's eyes.

She shakes her head.

" It would not amuse you, or, perhaps," with a blush, " it would amuse you too much ; and it would annoy me extremely. You will say good-bye now, I am sure," again making a confident proffer of her hand. This time he takes it.

" You have left me no other word to say," he answers rather ruefully.

She has lifted to his, in friendly farewell, the two chaste lamps of her clear serious eyes

—eyes well versed in tears, laughter, and tenderness, but unpractised in eye-manœuvre, or finesse; eyes ignorant of—or, if not, disdaining—the unused weapons in their armoury. Wolferstan looks back into them, down, down into their modest depths, to see whether no little devil lurks even at the very bottom of them.

But no! With an awe, slightly dashed by irritation, he has to own to himself, as he had to own at their last meeting at Dering, that he might be her grandfather. It is not often women look at him with such vestal eyes. Mostly he has found that the fire of his own, if not caught from women's eyes, has at least proved catching to them but the flame in Joan's might fitly burn on Dian's altar. Would it be a worthy, as it would undoubtedly be an agreeable task, to put out this vestal fire and light another, warmer, if not so clear? The idea is passing through his head, when she speaks and makes him ashamed of it.

"If you really came down from London, and subjected yourself to all the privations you told me of, only to see me—I wonder did you really?" in a parenthesis of girlish curiosity—"thank you very much for it. If not—if, as I believe, that is only a *façon de parler*, and you came down on some errand of your own—yet, still, thank you. I have thoroughly enjoyed seeing you."

He is very glad to hear it, but would have preferred that she should have been less able to tell him so.

"Do not say it in that solemn valedictory tone!" he answers, laughing lightly; "if you think that you are to be so easily quit of me you are mistaken. I have something of the gnat about me, I warn you! You always go to the shore in the morning, do not you?"

She smiles and raises her eyebrows a little.

"*Always!* why I have been here only two days."

"But you went there yesterday morning?"

" Yes."

" About eleven o'clock ?"

" Yes ?"

" And you went to-day ?"

" Yes."

" And you will go to-morrow ?" in a tone more affirmatory than interrogative.

" By all the laws of analogy !" she answers, breaking into a gay laugh, and so merrily takes leave.

CHAPTER X.

THE dogs, cantering on ahead of her, have apparently given Miss Dering's family notice of her approach, for, by the time she has reached the gate, she sees that they have all come out to meet her.

Mrs. Moberley, indeed, has advanced no farther than the door-step; but the girls are at the gate. One is holding it open : the other is peeping round the gate-post down the road. By the animation of their features and the unwonted sparkling of their eyes, it is clear that some more powerful motive than affection for their returning kinswoman has brought them out to meet her.

"We have such a piece of news for you!" cry they both in a breath; "we are not going to tell it you—you are to guess it—not that you ever will guess it!"

"And I have something for you—something belonging to you!" cries Bell, who is now discovered to be holding both hands behind her back. "Ah! if you knew what it was, you would not look so cool over it! say which hand—right or left?"

"Right," answers Joan laconically, and "right" it apparently is, for Miss Bell's plump hand unfolds itself to disclose a man's visiting card, upon which, on a closer survey, the name of "Colonel Wolferstan" is found to be legibly inscribed.

"Not a quarter of an hour after you were gone, he came," goes on Bell volubly; "I thought that of course it must be Micky—that no one else would call so early, and I was just on the point of running to open the door myself—just fancy if I had!"

"He had to ring four times before Sarah answered the bell," says Diana, taking up the wondrous tale ; " I was so much in hopes that he would have asked for mother, when he found that you were out ; but he did not : he asked, instead, where you had gone to ; and I heard Sarah telling him to Helmsley—what possessed her I cannot think ! it was just on the tip of my tongue to call out and say, 'No, she has not!' but I just stopped myself in time."

"We had a splendid view of him from behind the drawing-room blinds," says Bell in antistrophe ; " I could not have wished for a better !"

" Bell would put her head so far out of the window," cries Diana complainingly ; " say what I would to her ! he must have seen her —he could not have helped !"

" I know he did," rejoins Bell, colouring, but complacent ; " our eyes met : I felt that I went so red all in a minute !" After a pause : " If he is very anxious to see you, I should not wonder if he dropped in again later on ; do you think there is any likelihood of it ? do you think it is likely, Joan ? we may as well stay indoors all the afternoon on the chance."

" I would not if I were you," says Joan dryly ; " it would be labour lost ; if he had any anxiety to see me, it has been gratified, for he overtook me on the shore."

" And you have been sitting on the beach with him ?" cry both together, breathless and awe-struck.

" Yes."

" All this time ?"

" All this time."

" How I wish now that I had gone with you this morning !" cries Bell remorsefully ; " but who would have thought it ? all these years I have never met a creature on the shore—never !"

" You know I always said that I did not dislike the sea as much as you did ! did not I, Joan ?" says Diana in a tone of triumph, at having her toleration for the deep so signally justified.

"Is he there still, should you think?" says Bell in a rather languishing voice, and with her head slightly but sentimentally on one side; "did you leave him there? or did he come with you part of the way back?"

"Our road home was the same, you know!" answers Joan, blushing faintly; "so, of course, we came as far as the last stile together."

"Why did not you bring him into luncheon?" asks Mrs. Moberley hospitably; having, by this time, descended from the door-step and slowly advanced to join her family; "poor fellow! it would have been a charity—all alone in that big house! I think we might have kept his spirits up amongst us, eh, girls?"

"Thank God you did not!" says Diana in a devout aside; then in a louder key, "probably, mother, Joan bore in mind what you announced to us this morning, that there is nothing but a sheep's head for dinner!"

"No more there is!" says Mrs. Moberley contentedly; "the butcher is late with the meat as usual, so we have to make it out with odds and ends!"

"Fancy asking Anthony Wolferstan to sit down to a sheep's head!" cries Bell, laughing affectedly. "I should have expired!"

"I daresay that he has often sat down to a worse thing!" answers Mrs. Moberley sturdily. "Dear me! how a sheep's head does take me back to former times! how your poor father did love a sheep's head! never a week passed that we did not have one!"

"From all the anecdotes that you tell us of him, I think that father must have had rather gross tastes!" says Diana calmly.

"To think that a quarter of an hour should have made such a difference!" says Bell, still unable to tear herself from the original theme—"all the difference—if he had been a quarter of an hour earlier, or you had been a quarter of an hour later, he would have come in, and you would have been obliged to introduce him to us ; I must say that I should dearly like to know him, if it were only enough to be able to bow to him when we meet him in the road."

*　　*　　*　　*　　*

It is not often in April, and in the first half of April too, that one sees five consecutive days of honeyed warmth, and strong summer shining ; but it is so this year. The mighty young light next morning pouring into Joan's eyes, and waking her at an unearthly hour, when even the birds speak sleepily, shows her that not yet is there any lessening of the kingly beauty of the weather. Her first taste of the morning wind at her wide-flung window, tells her that there is no touch of shrewish east in it. She looks out yawningly towards her friend, the sea ; and so looking, ceases to yawn and smiles instead, at some recollection apparently.

"He is in the last link that connects me with civilisation," she says; "that is what gives him a factitious value; it would have been just as pleasant sitting there with any other of my old friends" (running over in her head a rather long list)—"yes—just as pleasant!" So saying she goes back to bed, and, still smiling, falls asleep again.

Later on, after breakfast, she is again wistfully eying the ocean; leaning against the gate-posts, surrounded by the dogs, who are asking as plainly as short excited barks and pathetically goggling eyes can ask, whether she is going out to walk, and if so, why she has not put her hat on. She is asking herself the same question. Shall she go to the sea-shore after all? Were Wolferstan still in London she undoubtedly would. Why then should she let his goings or comings influence or constrain hers? How winning the fresh fields would look! How

interesting it would be to see how much the
young wheat blades have sprung since this
time yesterday! and how many more marsh
marigolds have lit their brave gold fire by
the little swampy pool in the meadow!
And the sea! There is less wind to-day.
To-day there would be no white horses
tossing their snow-crests; no noisy breakers
riotously tumbling; only an unbounded
stretch of burnished silver, panting as in
some great love ecstasy.

She half closes her eyes, and with inward
vision longingly sees the unnumbered curves,
losing themselves in one another; the dreamy
ripple creeping to her feet; the green mer-
maid's hair afloat on the tide; the warm
sands, and across them Wolferstan, stepping
to meet her, with his low laugh, and his
welcoming eyes. At the thought of his, her
own re-open rather quickly.

"And you will go there to-morrow?"

The confidence of tone, the almost certainty
with which he spoke these words, re-echoes

in her ears. Why was he so sure that she would go? After all, what could Bell or Di do worse than hurry off at the first beck to meet their Bob or Micky at a given rendezvous?

"Now that I am poor, and of no reputation, I must hold my head a great deal higher, and more stiffly than I did in my palmy days! I will not go!" So saying, she turns resolutely away, and re-enters the house.

The dogs see that hope is extinct; and dropping their tails and voices, seek other avocations. Mr. Brown retires to the flower-bed, and begins to dig up a bone that he had wisely buried there yesterday, as a precaution against moments of ennui. Regy strolls down the road in search of one he loves; and of the other four, it is only needful to say that they have caught sight of the end of the tail of the Campidoglio cat. Indoors Joan finds all haste, bustle, and millinery. Early this morning arrived an unexpected summons

to bliss and barracks for the happy Misses
Moberley; at least, the next best thing to
barracks—a garden-party and dance afterwards, given by the Colonel's wife. By
superhuman exertions, by pressing into their
service every living thing on the premises,
the Misses Moberley hope that by four o'clock
in the afternoon their new alpacas will have
been fashioned into something so like a re-
semblance to one of Joan's gowns, as to
enable them, without too flagrant a violation
of truth, to tell their friends that they are
made on a Paris pattern. The establishment
being wholly female, every member of it,
without exception, is stitching. Even the
cook has been commanded to lay aside all
thoughts of pots and pans, and exchange her
professional skewer for a needle. For a few
moments Joan stands by in rueful silence
eying her martyred gown, which is being
pulled about, measured, pried into, unpicked
a little here and there. Then she conquers
herself and offers to help.

"Do you mean to say that you can sew?" asks Bell, with a little shrill laugh; "I should have thought that you were the sort of girl that would have been waited upon, hand and foot, and would never have set a stitch for yourself!"

"Appearances are deceitful then!" answers Joan quietly, sitting down, and settling resolutely to a long morning of feminine toil. And a very long morning it is. With no break of intervening dinner, it stretches away indeed into the afternoon. The room grows hot and the air confined, for Mrs. Moberley, having mislaid her big pair of scissors, no one is able to open the French window. By long stooping over her work, the blood not only seems to rush to her head, but to stay there. She drops her stitching at last, and lifts both hands to her hot forehead.

"I must say that it is rather hard upon Joan having all the work and none of the fun!" says Mrs. Moberley compassionately;

having herself come to a temporary pause in her labours, and being in the act of fanning herself with a sheet of the *Young Ladies' Journal;* "though, for my part, why you should not make one of us to-day, Joan, I cannot see; of course a grandfather would stand in the way of a public ball, or any such great formal do-ment—I am the last to say that he would not; but a little friendly frolic like this—no sit-down supper nor anything— nothing but ices and claret-cup, you may depend—and all got up in a moment too."

Joan shakes her head wearily.

"I had rather not, if you do not mind."

"Oh, please yourself, and you will please me!" rejoins Mrs. Moberley, waving the *Young Ladies' Journal* with a rather irritated air, "but I will say this, that who it is you take after I do not know. It certainly is not your poor mamma; she would have gone barefoot thirty miles any day for the chance of a *valse!*"

It is half-past four o'clock before the

Moberley family, having snatched a hasty
cold refreshment from a tray—having trium-
phantly endued the just finished alpacas—
stand ready to depart. Diana's head is surmounted by Micky's hat, from which the bird
of paradise's ample tail floats bold and
challenging as ever. It is too hot for Bobby's
jacket; so in this respect—having nothing to
correspond to the hat—Arabella labours
under an inferiority to her sister.

"I have seen worse-looking girls once or
twice, have not you, Joan?" says Mrs.
Moberley, regarding her offspring with a
playful complacency. "Quite the thing, I
declare! As soon as you are out of mourn-
ing—three months, or six, will it be? very
likely six, as you have got such a good stock
of black by you—but as soon as you are out,
I do not see why you should not all dress
alike. There is nothing that looks better
than three stylish girls pin for pin alike; they
set each other off."

They are gone now. With unfurled parasols

and flying ribbons, they are sailing gloriously down the road. Joan strolls into the garden, and standing on the broken pedestal of the old sun-dial, lays her hot cheek against the welcome coolness of its stained and ancient face. Then she lifts her head and reads again the short and half-effaced inscription, " Tempus fugit !"

" That must be my comfort," she says sighingly; " everything passes, nothing stays ! Let us do right, and whether happiness come or unhappiness, it is no very mighty matter. If it come, life will be sweet; if it do not come, life will be bitter—bitter, not sweet, and yet to be borne."

These brave words are not Joan's own. Still the very uttering of them makes her feel stronger. She puts on her hat and sets off for a long walk—not to the sea, however —she turns her back stoically upon it; tomorrow she will return thither. To-morrow the yellow sands will be again untrodden wastes, disturbed by no quick young foot,

probably, but her own.   But to-day she will
abstain.

She rambles aimlessly away with no other
guiding impulse than the desire to avoid
Helmsley, and the determination to keep
away from the ocean.   She follows the dogs'
noses more than any other leader.   Where
the rabbit scent is strongest thither they take
her.   After a while she finds herself in a
little still wood, alone.   Only the sound of
rustled leaves and a small squeaking bark of
utter excitement now and then, tell her that
her companions are still within hail, and are
in zealous pursuit of the ground game of
somebody unknown.

It would be a useless waste of voice to call
them, for they certainly would not obey.   So
with a sigh of content she sits down on the
warm dry leafy bed, and leans her still aching
head against the smooth stem of a young
beech-tree.   She has taken off her hat and
bared her forehead to the light handling of
the baby winds.   With a sense of deep

thorough peace and enjoyment, she looks
about her ; at the sticky horse-chestnut buds
beginning to break into crumpled leaf; at the
wood anemones, pure as snowdrops but not
half so cold, lifting their fine white heads and
delicate green collars ; at the primroses blos-
soming out in pale life from among the dead
oak-leaves, brown and curled.

Apparently, however, solitary peace is not
to be her portion for long. Not more than
five or ten minutes has she been resting in
dreamy tranquillity, when a step, heavier
than the dogs' light scampering patter,
troubles the quiet of the wood. Some game-
keeper, probably, justly irate at the invasion
of his covers and the disturbance of his
pheasants' eggs. Well, if she is to be scolded,
she may as well be scolded sitting as standing. So she neither rises nor changes her
position. With cheek leant against the
beech-bark, she awaits the oncomer's advent.
Nearer, nearer, the quick foot-falls come ; he
means to pass close beside her—he does not

mean to pass by her at all—he has stopped. With a half-frightened start she looks up. After all, she might as well have gone to the sea.

"No man can be more wise than destiny." It is Wolferstan!

CHAPTER XI.

"NOW about the laws of analogy?" he asks, taking off his hat, and looking rather angry; "what has become of them since yesterday?"

She looks up, smiling subtly.

"They are temporarily suspended."

The sweet carnation colour that surprise and half fright have sent flying up into her cheeks is kept prisoner there by pleasure.

After a moment: "Did you really expect to meet me there?" she asks.

Her smile is catching. A reflection of it brightens the young man's aggrieved features.

" If I had any self-respect I should answer
' no '; but as I have not, I will confess to you
that ' yes, I did !' "

" And you went there yourself ?"

" Of course."

" And waited some time ?"

" About two hours I should think," replies
the young man gravely ; " I built three large
sand castles, and saw two of them washed
away ; and I collected more cockle-shells
than I ever saw together in my whole life
before."

" Et puis ?"

" Puis—I gave it up as a bad job—particularly as I was becoming an object of
ridicule to three little boys and a nursery-
maid. Then I took my stand at that stile that
commands the Helmsley road and your house.
I thought, from the little I knew of you, that,
not even to avoid me, could you stay mewed
up indoors all such a day as this. Then I saw
the Misses Moberley and their mamma set
forth, arrayed like Solomon in all his glory.

Then I ventured a little nearer, and watched
you collect your dogs and set off; by-the-by,
may I sit down near you? at least a great
way off—just within ear-shot? or, if I do,
will you at once get up and walk away?"

She laughs a little.

"Do not be afraid! I am far too comfortable to stir."

"I stalked you stealthily," pursues Wolferstan, resuming his narrative; "I knew that
if I ventured to overtake you, you would turn
back, re-enter the house, and give me my
congé with as cold-blooded and inexorable a
gentleness as you did yesterday."

"You are very persistent!" she says,
looking at him with a slow serious smile;
"such perseverance, directed to worthier objects, might make you do great things."

"When one has come one hundred and
twenty miles to see one pair of—I mean to
attain one object," answers the young man,
emphasising his words by the steady fire of his
look, "one is hardly content to go away

without having succeeded, at least in some measure, in it."

The flush on Joan's face has hitherto amounted only to a fair cool pink; now it strengthens to a hot red glow of indignation, quite as beautiful to look at, but not nearly so comfortable to the wearer.

"May I beg of you not to make me any pretty speeches?" she says hurriedly; "I cannot tell you how they humiliate me! I never was fond of them in my good days—never; but now—now I dislike them far more than ever I did!" (giving one blue flash out of her eyes at him, and then hastily looking away). "If I were an unsophisticated country girl of seventeen, I could understand your thinking that they would please me; but I am surprised at your imagining that a woman who has been three—nearly four years in the world—your own world should be so credulous!"

"I stand reproved!" answers Wolferstan quietly; "I am aware that in society it is nearly as rude to tell a person that you like them as that you dislike them. I withdraw the obnoxious statement; I came down to see that the rooms were kept properly aired."

She smiles a little against her will.

" If you really mean to be a friend to me," she continues presently, in a rather appeased tone, and looking at him with the direct and open honesty of her eyes; "and, indeed, I am very willing that you should be so—I am not so rich in them that I can afford to throw away one—but if you do, will you promise to treat me exactly as you would a man-friend ? You would not—" (blushing again a little, but quite slightly and pleasantly) — " you would not compliment a man-friend on the colour of his eyes, would you ?"

He laughs.

" Probably not."

" Then exercise the same forbearance towards me !" she says gaily yet earnestly; " if you do, it will put me into much better humour both with myself and you; will you promise me—will you?"

"Promise to look upon you as a man?" says Wolferstan, leaning his back against a stalwart oak, that, as yet, holds forth no sign of summer clothing, and answering her with a gravity equal to her own; "no, I do not think I can; if you knew what men are, you would not wish me to do so!—promise to refrain from pretty speeches to you?— willingly!"

"It is a bargain then!" she cries merrily, stretching out her hand frankly to him; "let us shake hands upon it! but mind—at the first complimentary allusion to the shape of my nose, or the colour of my hair, our friendship dissolves; smashed, splintered into a thousand fragments."

"And now," says Wolferstan, laughing gaily, and diminishing by a couple of yards the space that he had at first ostentatiously put between them; "now that you have prescribed your conditions, I am going to prescribe—no ! that is much too courageous a word—going meekly to suggest mine !"

She smiles a little suspiciously.

" It is a thousand pounds to one penny that I do not accept them !"

" Let us suppose that you are the man-friend that you are so anxious to be, and that I am not at all anxious that you should be, and that I had made an appointment to meet you in Pall Mall, to which you had agreed, would you at once set off for Seven Dials ?"

She laughs mischievously.

" I think it is more than probable."

" You are forgetting that you are man," says Wolferstan gravely, " and that the privilege of snapping your fingers at common sense and producing effects without causes is wholly feminine."

" Then I will not be a man !" she cries a little petulantly ; " away with my toga virilis. I resume my distaff."

" If I am to be a friend," continues Wolferstan more earnestly, and beating out his proposition with the forefinger of one hand on the palm of the other, " I will not be treated as an enemy—there is no logic in it ; I will not be suspected and shunned ! What harm " (speaking more quickly and eagerly, and looking into her attentive face)—" what harm do you think I am planning you ? As I live, I have no thought or wish but for your good and pleasure—and my own !" (in a lowered voice, with an afterthought of candour). "Placed as we are—as chance has placed us, we may considerably sweeten each other's lives ; why, in Heaven's name, should not we ?"

Her eyes are fixed in grave inquiry, asking for explanation, on his, but she says nothing.

" Do not think," he continues, " that I over-rate my own worth in your eyes, or that I think that you see charms in me, which you have never given me reason to suppose that you do ; if the old state of things still continued, I am aware that I should have no value at all—I should be one of a mob, as I always used to be; but now, as you said yesterday, I am the last fragment left of the good old life—your last connecting link with civilisation—is it not so?"

Her eyelids droop over her sad eyes.

"Yes," she says sighingly.

"Any society procurable *there*," he goes on, indicating by a gesture the direction where Helmsley smoke, turned gold by the sun, hangs against the sky, "I warn you beforehand, you will not be able for one moment to tolerate."

"You are mistaken," she answers resolutely; "henceforth I do not mean to allow myself any fine lady squeamishness. I wince now, because these are early days; by-and-by I shall not wince."

He shakes his head.

"You have been transplanted too late; you will never take kindly to the soil."

An expression of pain crosses her face.

"If it is so, what is the use of telling me?" she cries reproachfully. "I am *in* the soil,

and whether I flourish or whether I wither,
here I must stay, at least for the present."
After a moment's pause : "I had rather not
talk about it ; things talked about and dis-
cussed gain a substance and importance that
they never have when they are not put into
words. Things that must be, must ; if you"
(looking at him with a slightly satirical
smile) "were to fall down from your high
estate you would find that it would not kill
you ; you would find yourself alive at the
bottom of the hill. I have found myself
alive."

A silence—at least as much silence as there
ever can be in a spring wood.

Some of the dogs have come back, and
now lie on the leafy primrosy bed, with their
fawn-sides heaving and their tongues hanging
out sideways surprisingly far. Mr. Brown,
whose increasing embonpoint has told upon
his wind, lays his puckered face on Joan's
black lap, and falls sweetly, if snoringly, asleep.

Joan's eyes are fixed on a spot where,

through the still bare oak-boughs, she can
see a nation of Lent lilies spreading over a
neighbouring field : fair Lent lilies—April
fine ladies with their pale yellow gowns and
their deeper yellow petticoats. Her heart is
echoing Wolferstan's words: "You will never
take kindly to the soil." No, never. She
will always be a blanched sickly plant, like a
geranium in a town cellar. What is it that
gives her this sense of well-being, of smooth
comfort and pleasure, in Wolferstan's society?

As far as wisdom is concerned, any or all
of his remarks might have been uttered by
Micky Brand; nor has he needed reprimanding
for over-civility less than did that other hero.
And yet how soothed—how much at home
she feels with him. The certainty of immu-
nity from underbred jests, of having her
allusions understood, and of being on the
same plane of thought make her feel that,
though an inscrutable destiny has poured
blood of the same quality into her veins and
those of the Moberleys, yet that by every

law of affinity she is much more nearly akin
to the young man lying in the gold sunshine
at her feet. Advantages in him, which before
had passed unnoticed—taken for granted—
now start out in delightful prominence. The
quality of his voice—the purity of his pro-
nunciation—these it is which contrast so
blessedly with the loud and twangy pro-
vincialisms of her relatives—her relatives—
whose every laugh, yawn, sneeze sets her
teeth on edge.

The object of her thoughts breaks in upon
them by saying :

"My people will be down here by the end
of July; they generally stay here most of
the autumn. I do not at all promise that
you will like them. My father, poor old
man, is not in a condition to be either liked
or disliked, as perhaps you have heard; and
my mother—no" (with a little reflective
smile)—"I cannot even promise that you will
be very much delighted with her, but they
mostly have the house full of pleasant people;

and if you will let us hold out the right hand of fellowship to you, I think we may make your life a shade more endurable. Of course" (with a slight shrug) " if you resolutely set up your quills against us, we can do nothing."

She shakes her head.

" If you are a fish," she says a little doggedly, " it is best to stay in the water; if a bird, in the air. If you have sunk to a lower level, it is wiser to keep to it, and not to be standing on tiptoe straining up to the heights you have left."

He looks a little disappointed.

" You refuse the right hand of fellowship, then ?"

" No, I do not," she says sorrowfully. " If I were wise I should; but I suppose that one is greedy of pleasure. Most likely if your mother holds it out, I shall snatch at it; but" (in a lighter tone) "she has not done so yet. It will be time enough to talk about it when she does."

Another silence; a silence gently dreamily sad on the part of the girl; pleasantly and rather affectionately reflective on the part of the man; serenely somnolent on the part of the dogs. As usual, the dogs have the best of it. It is broken at last by Joan, not because she wishes to speak or has anything special to say, but because she feels that, however great may be the strides that her intimacy with Wolferstan has lately taken, she does not yet know him well enough to sit beside him in that total silence which is the privilege only of perfect friendship or assured love.

"Are you down here—I mean, at the Abbey—much?" she asks presently.

He shakes his head and stretches out a lazy hand to pat Mr. Brown's fat flank.

"Not much; not nearly so much as I should be, only that whenever I do come down mother and I always manage to fall out about one and the same subject. The fact is" (laughing slightly, and looking with a faintly-heightened colour at the girl's serene face)—"the fact is, that she is always worrying me to marry; why, I cannot understand, as in any case she has my brother to fall back upon: a rangé gray-headed boy, who, unlike me, never follows wandering fires."

"And you do not feel able to oblige her?" asks Joan, with an expression of friendly interest, looking back at him with a perfectly unembarrassed smile, which, unknown and certainly unconfessed to himself, rather annoys him.

Again he shakes his head, and laughs.

"To my thinking the laws of marriage require a good deal of modification before they are adapted to the needs of so advanced a civilisation as ours." A moment later, speaking with an almost irritated quickness and eagerness: "What, in Heaven's name, is it about you that makes me, against my will, admit to you truths that I know will lower me in your estimation? Perhaps" (laughing a little restlessly)—"perhaps if you sat with your back to me I might lapse into my usual gently inventive vein. I think it is your eyes that——no——" (seeing her hold up her finger in warning)—"it is no infringement of our bargain—it is nothing complimentary—rather the reverse—to tell you that your eyes are rigidly truthful and truth-compelling."

"Perhaps it will be safer to abstain from any remarks at all about them," answers Joan, with a rather cold smile. " Let us suppose that I have no eyes."

"With all my heart," rejoins he, laughing. " Five minutes ago we agreed that you were a man, now you are a blind man. I shudder to think of what you may become in the course of the next five minutes." Another pause; then Wolferstan resumes with some heat his original theme. " Imagine swearing to love any woman, or, in a woman's case, any man, half a century hence, as warmly as you do now; when I look back ten years and see how in that short space every idea, feeling, opinion is changed or modified, how can I expect that at the end of fifty or sixty years one remnant of the original *I* will be left? Half a century! always opposite the same face, always fond, always faithful, it is" (throwing his eyes upward to the brown tree roof above him)—" it is a monstrous thing to ask of any human being."

He looks at Joan in half-laughing, half-serious appeal, but neither eyes nor mouth give him any hint of her agreement or disagreement. The one is shut, the others are down-dropped to the primroses in her lap, and with her fingers she is lovingly stroking their downy stalks.

" One might as well," pursues the young man, beginning to curl Mr. Brown's tail (relaxed in slumber) round his finger, and thereby waking and vexing him—"one might as well swear to have all one's teeth in one's jaws or all one's hair on one's head at the end of the same period; the one seems to me quite as much within one's own power as the other."

Still no word or sign of assent or dissent.

"When I say a thing," continues the young man, speaking more gravely, while the faithless light of his gray eyes steadies to a more serious shining—"I mean, when I say it soberly and solemnly, I like to be able to persuade at least myself that I mean it, and am going to stick to it. If" (reddening a little)—"if I, as I now am, were to swear to love any one woman wholly and exclusively for the rest of my natural life, I should feel that I was the most consummate ruffian in existence; for I should know that I was swearing a lie! do you now see why I cannot oblige my mother?"

She nods slightly.

"Yes, I see!"

She has risen to her feet, and so stands tall and willowy. The flame-eyed west sun is boldly kissing her swart clothes and her milky throat and her red lips; and the ruffed anemones are crowding about her feet.

"And you think that I am right?" cries the young man, eagerly snatching, as if involuntarily, at the hand that, loosely drooping by her side, hangs nearest to him, and locking it, with all its crushed primroses, in his firm young clasp.

"I think," she says, with a slow soft smile, while her blue eyes rest gently, coolly, sweetly, on the restless fire of his—"I think that a day will come when you will change your tune; when you will blame the fifty years for being too short, not too long; at least, for your sake, I hope that it will!"

CHAPTER XII.

"IT seems to be always good-bye!" Wolferstan is saying a little ruefully.

Together they have strolled slowly home through the dew-crisped meadows. Together they have watched the sun's nightly swoon; what so quickly rises again into life, cannot be called death; and praised his parting benediction to the courtier clouds.

Together they now stand in the dusty road at the gate of Portland Villa. Joan smiles soberly.

" 'How do you do?' would lose all his charm

—specially in men's eyes—if they did not know that his brother 'Good-bye' treads so hard upon his heels."

"They are not come back yet," says Wolferstan, surveying with his eyes the front of the house—silent windows, and closed door; "if they were" (smiling), "I feel sure that I should see some indication of them, as I did yesterday morning."

"I did not expect them," answers Joan; "they have gone to a dance; they will not be back till two or three o'clock."

"And you will be alone all evening?"

"Yes."

"And" (in a rather lowered voice)—"and I shall be alone all evening!"

"Yes."

If he had contemplated proposing any plan that should entail their not being alone all evening, something, either in her face or in her "yes," makes him change his mind.

"Which is your window?" he asks, lifting his eyes to the upper story. "I should be

sorry to mistake Mrs. Moberley's for it; I
shall be passing by to-morrow morning on
my way to the station before you are awake;
and though I shall see only your blinds—"

"You will certainly not see them," answers
Joan, laughing; "for I have none; they fell
to pieces ten years ago, and have never since
been replaced."

A moment's silence. The wind is making
a soft sighing bustle in the hedge, and the
distant Helmsley churches chime eight.

"You will not send me a line now and
then, I suppose?" suggests Wolferstan diffidently, leaning on the gate.

"Certainly not."

"Not even if you are in any trouble?"

"I cannot imagine any trouble in which
you would be able to help me," she answers
gravely; "if I were sick, I could not ask you
to nurse me; if I were starving, I could not
ask you for bread."

"Then why call me friend?" cries the
young man hotly; "what is the use of an

empty name in which there is no meaning ?"

She smiles a little teasingly.

" As you say, what use ?—let us drop it !"

" If," continues the young man eagerly—
" if, by-and-by—not very soon—I run down
again to—to—see whether the rooms are kept
aired " (laughing a little)—" will there be
any chance—is it likely that—that the laws
of analogy will have resumed their sway ?"

" Do you mean," she answers, smiling, yet
gravely, while her look meets his, full-eyed
and collected—" do you mean shall I be likely
to make appointments to meet you on the
shore?—most assuredly not!—I know nothing
more unlikely; if we meet accidentally—really
accidentally — not accidentally on purpose "
(laughing)—" I shall be delighted ; I like to
see you : it gives me pleasure ; as I have told
you till you must be tired of hearing it, you
are the last connecting link between me and
my good old life !"

He makes an impatient gesture with his

foot, which, had he been a child, would have been called a stamp.

"I am tired of being a link," he says petulantly; "I will not be a link any longer! it sounds as if I were a high-class ape! when —in how much time—shall I stand upon my own merits? in how many months—years— will you be glad to see me because I am *I*, and for no tedious second reasons?"

"Ah, when?" she echoes playfully; and so, with no further good-bye, quietly eludes him, and slipping through the gate and into the house, disappears.

*   *   *   *   *

It is next morning. Wolferstan is gone, and has taken the summer weather with him. It is not the sun that wakes her to-day; but the sound of Wolferstan's wheels, rolling sharply through her dreams. Cautiously hidden behind her curtains, so that not a tip of nose or end of eyelash may be seen, she watches him bowl past; while the chill rain drives into his eyes, tries to put out his cigar, and blurs his last view of Mrs. Moberley's window, at which he is mistakenly gazing.

By the time she is dressed and downstairs the day has made up its mind to be regularly wet; no shilly-shallying half-measures! The panes are already streaming, the wind whistles instead of sighing; the young flowers shiver and shrink, and the dogs, having been lured to the front gate by the insulting noises made in passing by a butcher's boy, trot back wiht lowered tails, shaking their coats and sneezing.

The house appears quite empty, though certainly neither " swept " nor " garnished." Not a soul above nor below stairs shows signs of life. For the early part of the day she will probably be companionless, as the Moberley family are repairing by sleep the ravages of yesternight's dissipation.

To be equally without occupation ; to have no other employment than to sit with idle hands, wondering to what station on his

London route Wolferstan has yet attained, is out of the question.

"I never used to wonder how far he was on his journey," she says to herself with a sort of surprise, standing at the window looking out at the sickly cypresses bowing in the gale, listening to the moaning of the rainladen sea wind. "When he was gone, he was gone—and there was an end of him! there *must* be an end of him now."

Resolutely so saying, she turns away at once from the window, and, stepping lightly and softly past the Moberleys' doors, mounts to the lumber room at the top of the house, whither most of her big boxes have been relegated. From one of them she extracts an armful of books, and carrying them downstairs with her, buries herself in them.

It is past mid-day before the Misses Moberley and their parent, yawning, pale, *désœuvrées*, with sketchy toilet details, and heavy eyelids, make their appearance. Evidently incapable of any other occupation than reminiscence, they throw themselves into the three soundest and easiest chairs that the flimsily furnished room affords.

" It was *heavenly*," says Bell, with a prodigious emphasis, in answer to an inquiry from her cousin as to how they had enjoyed themselves. " How I wish it could all come over again ! All of *them* were there, and nearly half another regiment from Kingsford besides. I am sure that I might have danced every dance three times over ; so might Di !"

" That was only because there were so few girls," says Diana bluntly ; " they had had a great many disappointments ; that was why they sent off post haste for us at the last moment."

" I cannot think, Di," cries Mrs. Moberley fretfully, " why you always seem to have such a pleasure in taking the gilt off our gingerbread. Do you know, Bell," with a sudden change in the current of her ideas—" do you know, Bell, it strikes me that they must have had the whole supper, just as it stood, from

Tucker in the High Street—only the soups to be heated up, you know. A pretty penny it must have cost them. I never saw anything better done in my life—no stint anywhere, and the champagne corks flying the whole of the night."

" I daresay," answers Bell indifferently ; " of course the supper is everything to you, but I do not care about it myself; I am always far too excited to eat." After a moment : " You really must come next time, Joan ! You need not be afraid of any lack of partners ; it will be pick and choose with you, and, indeed, they are all on the alert to see you already. We have given such a glowing description of you —you may trust us for that !"

" Indeed, Joan, there is no reason why you should mew yourself up," says Mrs. Moberley, joining in assentingly, " a fine showy girl like you ! Better make hay while the sun shines," laughing, " in a white gown with a black sash, and black shoes and black ornaments ;

if you do not happen to have any, Di has got a pair of gutta-percha bracelets that she could lend you. No one would think of expecting more of you than that, particularly," dropping her voice to a very low key, " particularly under the circumstances !"

Joan makes no reply beyond a very small shake of the head, and a still smaller smile. When the battle has to be fought really, she has no doubt of having strength enough and to spare for it, but now it would be waste of fibre—there being no warlike dissipation, and therefore no need for evading it this afternoon.

" And you ?" says Bell, stretching out both arms, and laying her limp head back on the chair-cushion ; " how did you manage to get through the evening—you slept, I daresay ? No more adventures on the beach, I suppose ?"

" I did not go there."

" Then you saw nothing more of Anthony Wolferstan, I suppose ? *Anthony !* — dear me, what a lovely name it is ! How I wish

that I knew him well enough to call him
Anthony!"

To Joan's wonder and immeasurable disgust and sorrow, she feels herself blushing:
feels the slow red burning grow and strengthen
in her cheeks. For once in her life she would
give one or both her ears to be able to tell a
lie; but now, as ever, it is impossible to her.

" I walked in the other direction," she
answers, with a collected, if crimson, gravity,
" to a wood—I do not know its name—but
he happened to overtake me."

" *Happened!*" echoes Mrs. Moberley in a
raised key, and with a roguishly rallying
smile, while Diana stops in mid-yawn, and
Bell lifts her languid lolling head with suddenly revived animation; "we all know what
kind of ' happened' that is—do not we, girls?
So, after all, Miss Joan, it seems that you
are as much up to a little bit of mischief as
the others!"

Unused to this kind of banter, hating it
past the power of any words to express,

feeling the tears rising in her throat, and
trying to swallow them back, Joan sits in
red misery, as complete a picture of discomfiture in a small way as the world can afford.
Taking perhaps her dumbness for the silence
of enjoyment, or else too much pre-occupied
with her own merriment to give a thought
to the subject of Joan's feelings, Mrs. Moberley is already preparing for more badinage,
when Di gallantly rushes to the rescue.

"What a pile of books you have there,
Joan!" she cries, with abrupt compassion
changing the subject, taking up a volume
and looking at its title-page; "no wonder
that the carrier complained of the weight of
your boxes."

> "'When land is gone, and money spent,
>   Then learning is most excellent!'"

answers Joan, recovering her countenance
and her self-command, and looking gratefully
back at her cousin; "as" (smiling a little
sadly)—"as my whole fortune lies in my
brains, I like to know how large it is; if, as

is most probable, I shall have to be a governess, it is as well to know what I can teach!"

"Governess!" echoes Mrs. Moberley, with
a brusque heartiness; "fiddlesticks' ends,
and fried eggs! You have no more need to
be governess than Bell or Di have; the only
difference is that now I have three daughters
instead of two; three little pigs to drive to
market" (with a comfortable chuckle). "If
your own flesh and blood (and what *can*
be well nearer than an *aunt?*) cannot board
and lodge you at a pinch, things *are* come to
a pretty pass."

"I would not be a governess," cries Bell,
throwing up her eyes to the well-smoked
ceiling, and shrugging her shoulders, "no—
not for anything you could give me! If we
were reduced in circumstances that is the very
last thing that I should ever think of turning
my hand to."

"How servants do despise governesses,"
pursues Mrs. Moberley, sliding into placid
reminiscence; "I remember what trouble we

used to have with ours when we were girls; the button-boy never would answer her bell when she rang; and the cook always forgot to send up her supper. I declare, Bell," (with a sudden change of tone from calm recollection of the past to warm excitement in the present)—" I declare, Bell, if those pigs are not in the garden again—there never was anything like the cleverness of a pig about opening gates."

So saying, as quickly as the peculiarities of her form will allow, and followed by her eldest daughter, she hurries out of the room.

Diana and Joan remain behind, in silence at first; then Di speaks:

" Were you joking, or are you going to be a governess, really ?"

" Really."

" You will not like it."

"No, I know that I shall not," replies Joan; her eyes absently fixed on the figure of her aunt, as seen through the window, in waterproof and clogs, with arms extended

like a windmill, splashing through the puddles
in pursuit of the alien swine. " But you
think " (with a short uneasy laugh and
painful blush)—" that *that*—that anything,
in fact—would be better than—than—*us!*"

Joan looks uncomfortable.

" I think," she says gently, " that no
young, able-bodied person, who can earn
their own bread, has any business to be
eating other people's all their days."

" Taine's ' Nouveaux Essais de Critique et
d'Histoire,' " says Diana, slowly spelling out
one of the titles. " You are not reading
them for pleasure then ?" (in a relieved voice).
" I thought you could not be."

Joan laughs.

" They expect so much from governesses
nowadays," resumes Diana presently. " Do
you mean to say" (in a rather awed tone)
" that you think you are up to the mark ?"

" That is what I want to find out."

" We are grossly ignorant," resumes the
other candidly ; " grossly. The other day—

in the winter, Bobby—Bell's Bobby, you know—offered to lend us a French novel. We took it, because we did not like to own that we could not read it; but we could not" (shaking her head)—"we could not make head or tail of it."

"Shall I teach you?" cries Joan eagerly. "Will you be my first pupil? the first victim of my inexpertness? Do—I am quite serious; it would be a boon to me, and—"

"Go back into the school-room again," cries Diana, opening her eyes widely in surprise at this proposition; "why, Bell and I were finished two years ago; I was nineteen last February; many people are married at nineteen : several of our schoolfellows were—one had a baby."

"But you are not married!" replies Joan, again laughing; "and until that blest epoch arrives—"

"It never will," replies Diana solemnly and sorrowfully, shaking her head; "who would marry *us?*" she says, with a sincere self-scorn. "Do we look like the sort of girls that men *marry?*—it never struck me in that light till you came, but now I see that we are fit to be nothing but camp-followers! I believe that I must have been born in a baggage-wagon!"

"Must you?" with a rather embarrassed smile.

"Even if I shaved my fringe," continues Diana gravely, pulling it out over her eyes, and squinting awfully in the endeavour to see it; "even if I daily dipped my head into a bucket of cold water to flatten it, it would never look like yours—would it now? Speak truth—gospel truth."

But Joan is happily saved from the necessity of replying to this difficult and delicate query.

"They were the Sardanapalus pigs!" cries Mrs. Moberley in a raised key, re-entering the room, flushed with victory, and casting off her waterproof like a tight husk; "luckily it is easy to know them—they are the only Berkshire ones in the row."

CHAPTER XIII.

MONTH has crawled away since Joan rang her first timid peal at the bell at Portland Villa. Months have as many different paces as any other time-measures. Some gallop wildly; some trot smartly; some creep on all-fours. This one has been among the slowest paced. Now it is gone; and—insipidly unpleasant as it has been—there is no reason for rejoicing at its being over; for, as far as human eye can see, as far as human reason can judge, the brothers that, indefinitely numerous, tread upon its heels are not at all likely to be

more agreeable; except inasmuch as use hardens people to the uncongenial and the unlovely. And the power of use, in this respect, has, Joan is beginning to think, been overrated. Use—twenty-eight, nay thirty days' use—has failed at all to reduce her shrinking from rumpled stain-freaked table-cloths; at all to decrease her desire furtively to wipe her dull tea-spoon before putting it between her lips; in the least degree to lessen the wonder of the problem how Mrs. Moberley came to be her aunt; or in any measure to increase her fondness for amative military jokes—jokes, not *by* the soldiers—let us do them that justice—but about them.

It is mid-May now, but mid-May not as poets sing it, but with its lovely face puckered and pinched by the spiteful nipping of the east winds. They have been nipping, pinching, withering for a full week past, and they are nipping, pinching, withering still. Joan, standing by the propped-open window of her little room, and leaning her head against the paintless frame, is looking musingly out, and running over in her mind the little bald incidents of the last four weeks. Thrice the butcher has forgotten, or at least omitted to bring the meat. Twice Sarah has let fall the tray and smashed four of the soundest cups and saucers and six of the healthiest plates. Three times the ingenious pigs have lifted the latch and re-entered the garden. Five times there have been warlike gaieties to be staved off; each time successfully, but also each time after a harder battle and giving more offence. Twenty—nay, it is impossible to count how many times—Micky Brand has been here, and Wolferstan has been here not at all! At thought of the first of these two names, she, being alone, makes a gesture of impatience and distaste : at thought of the last, she turns away from the window, and taking up a little almanac from the table examines it. Twenty-eight days — exactly four weeks—since they shook hands by that gate, between the waning sun and waxing moon, and he humbly asked permission to come soon again.

She laughs a little derisively. Thank God she did not give it—did not give that unnecessary leave. To grant a favour of which the recipient does not think it worth his while to avail himself is one of the most considerable among the minor humiliations to which flesh is liable. When one is severed from any state of existence it is useless to try and hang on to it by a single thread. And yet, probably, she herself would hardly have had the courage to cut the thread; Wolferstan has kindly done it for her.

"As I am now henceforth and for ever one of the bourgeoisie—one of the minor bourgeoisie," she says, relentlessly putting her fate into words, "it certainly is as well that I should receive as few as possible of a fine gentleman's idle attentions ; particularly" (smiling bitterly) "as he took such pains to explain to me that they were only idle."

So saying, she takes up a book and buries

herself in it until the hour devoted to Diana's instruction shall strike. For Diana has proved herself superior to the force of public opinion—the public opinion of her own circle and family—and triumphing over, not only her own sense of the unseemliness of voluntarily resuming those leading-strings which two years ago she so joyfully cast away, but over Bell's persistent persiflage, and proving herself invulnerable even by the darts of Micky's wit, now daily sits at the feet of her new Gamaliel, and looks forward hopefully to the time when the next French novel shall be offered for her acceptance, and she will be able proudly to take it, and ostentatiously to enjoy its now occult beauties.

To Joan the two hours devoted to this task are the most bearable in the day. Each exercise of patience, called forth by Diana's dulness; each small slow victory over ignorance and misapprehension, seems to her a step towards the desired goal of independence and self-maintenance.

If she can teach Diana, she can teach
others, though seldom, probably, will she
meet with a pupil who, to so deep a consciousness of her own shortcomings, unites
so honest a determination to be ultimately
very learned. The course of study has this
morning been in full swing for about half an
hour, when Joan perceives, by the wandering
of Diana's eyes, the wavering of her colour,
and the additional stumbling with which she
begins to jog through Racine's classic page,
that some outside object is distracting her
attention.

"What is it?" she cries a little impatiently;
"how you are murdering it!"

"It is Micky," replies Diana rosily.

"Is that all?" says Joan carelessly; "I
thought that at least it must be the rag and
bone man! Well,

"'Que vois-je? est-ce Hermione? et que viens je d'entendre?
Pour qui coule le sang que je viens de répandre?'"

Diana complies:

17—2

"'Que vois-je ? est-ce Hermione ? et que viens je d'entendre ?

Pour qui coule le sang que je viens de répandre ?'"

But having rendered Orestes' horror-struck question with as little surprise and as much tameness as it is well possible, she again stops. "You do not think that we need go down, then ?"

"Certainly not !" replies Joan shortly; "how many people does he need to entertain him ? he has two already—your mother and Bell."

"That is true," says Diana, with an air of reluctant conviction, again limpingly resuming the heroic frenzy of the son of Agamemnon :

"'Je suis, si je l'en crois, un traître, un assassin !

Est-ce Pyrrhus qui meurt ? et suis-je Oreste enfin ?'"

The house-door has been opened. Micky's weighty foot has been heard along the passage : a louder buzz of talk below tells of the fillip he is giving to the conversation.

"You do not think that he will take it unkind ?" suggests Diana, again breaking off.

" It is not of the least consequence if he does."

" No, of course not " (with a sigh).

" ' Quoi j'etouffe en mon cœur la raison qui m'éclaire.
   J'assassine à regret un roi que je révère ;
   Je viole en un jour le droit des souverains,
   Ceux des ambassadeurs.' "

" You are to come downstairs at once, both of you," cries Bell, who, during the previous lines, having been heard noisily scampering up the carpetless stairs, now bursts into the room, and—both chairs being occupied—falls out of breath on the bed.

" Who says so ?" asks Joan quickly, growing angrily pink.

" Mother," replies Bell, panting and affectedly holding her hand to her heart ; " she has been telling Micky about your singing, Joan, and how your ' Barbara Allen ' made her cry last night. He says " (laughing) "that he wants to see whether you can make him cry too !"

For the twentieth time Joan regrets the

visit of a passing tuner, who, by exercising
his skill on the cracked old spinet, and restoring their voices to its half a dozen dumb
notes, has taken away her best excuse for
not trotting forth her accomplishment for
the benefit of Mrs. Moberley's warlike
friends.

Diana has already jumped up, and letting
Orestes and his frenzy roll on the floor, is
standing before the glass, smoothing and
beautifying her wild hair with one of Joan's
brushes.

The drawing-room door, when opened, dis-
closes Micky stretched at easy length upon
the sofa, not offering to help Mrs. Moberley,
who is already opening the dusty piano, and
trying to infuse a little steadiness into the
uncertain music-stool.   He is indeed occupied
in trying to teach Mr. Brown the well-known
accomplishment of "Trust and paid for;"
whereof Mr. Brown fully understands and
appreciates the last half, but can see neither
humour nor point in the first.   Joan's en-

trance frees him from the strain of education, for in a moment his teacher is off the sofa, and advancing with some demonstrativeness to meet her. He is indeed so much occupied by his salutation to his new friend as to omit taking any notice of his old one, which he afterwards gracefully explains and apologises for by saying that he had quite forgotten that he had not seen her before.

"You did not know that I was here, I suppose," he says, confidently glancing from one girl to the other; "did not expect me so early?"

Diana looks foolish; but Joan answers coldly and serenely:

"We saw you coming up the drive."

"They were at lessons," cries Bell, giggling; "two good little girls with their primers and copy-books."

"Have you got to pothooks and hangers yet?" asks Micky jocosely; but his wit is thrown away upon the object at which it is wholly aimed, as she has joined her aunt at the piano, and is listening to her cautions with regard to the music-stool.

"If you do not lean your whole weight upon it, and if you do not screw it up too high, I think it will hold," she says, gravely testing it with one hand. In obedience to this advice Joan sits gingerly down, and forthwith strikes up the dear old ditty :

"In Scarlet town, where I was born,
    There was a fair maid dwelling,
  Made ev'ry youth cry well-a-away;
    Her name was Barbara Allen.

"All in the merry month of May,
    When green buds they were swelling,
  Young Jemmy Grove on his death-bed lay,
    For love of Barbara Allen.

"Then slowly, slowly she came up,
    And slowly she came nigh him,
  And all she said when there she came,
    'Young man, I think you're dying.'"

Mr. Brand has stationed himself close behind the performer, with his thumb and forefinger on the score, in the full intention of whipping the leaf smartly over as soon as her voice arriving at *ing* shall warn him that it is time. In this well-meant but ill-executed

endeavour he only succeeds in felling the
music-book to earth. As they both stoop to
pick it up he says to her in a loud clumsy
whisper from among the legs of the piano :

" ' Young man, I think you're dying ;'
that is just what I can fancy you saying."

For all answer, she hastily resumes her lay :

" When he was dead and laid in grave,
Her heart was struck with sorrow."

"That is the hall-door bell!" cries Diana,
interrupting, and pricking up her ears;
"surely!"

"Only the area!" answers Bell, shaking
her head; "they are so like — three times
this morning it has taken me in!"

" Oh mother, mother, pity me !
For I shall die to-morrow."

Mrs. Moberley has taken out her pocket-
handkerchief, being sure that she will soon
feel inclined to cry. Regy has half lifted
his nose : not quite sure whether the suffering
inflicted on him by Miss Dering's melody is
acute enough to justify a howl; and Micky

has replaced his no-longer-needed thumb and forefinger in his pocket.

But Barbara Allen is fated not to die to-day. Her death agonies are interrupted by the appearance of Sarah, who now noisily enters; her face capriciously freaked with smuts; and in her hand a bouquet of choice hot-house flowers, which, with a forethought and self-consciousness of dirt not to be too much commended, she is shielding from contact with her dusky fingers, by the interposition of a portion of the tail of her hardly less dusky gown. Flowers such as used to be Joan's daily bread : flowers such as she never sees now save in envious dreams. In a moment she is off the music-stool. In a moment they are all up and out of their chairs, and crowding round Sarah.

" Where are they from ?"

" For whom are they ?"

" Who brought them ?"

" As sure as fate it is Jackson !" cries Bell, with a rapturous simper; " the idea of his daring—and I told him as plainly as I could speak that he was not to do anything of the kind—the youngest subaltern in the regiment!"

Di's big blue eyes are fixed rather wistfully with a faint hope upon Micky's face; but, alas! there is no consciousness on that large and bovine expanse.

" If you please, 'm," says Sarah, as soon as they will allow her to speak—conscientiously holding the nosegay at arm's length, in order to be able to resist the almost irresistible temptation to sniff its perfume; " if you please, 'm, I was to say that they are for Miss Joan, from the *H*abbey !"

" From the Abbey !" cries Bell in a disgusted tone, falling back into her chair, and turning as many colours as a dead mackerel; " then it is not Jackson after all !"

" Is the Colonel down ? did he bring them himself ? when did he come ?" cries Mrs. Moberley, volleying question after question; while the fatness of her cheeks is unable wholly to veil the triumphant fire of her eyes.

"It was not the Colonel, 'm; it was one of the grooms!" answers Sarah, delivering up the flowers into their owner's most ready hands, and retreating to the door.

"Did you give him a glass of beer? I hope you gave him a glass of beer!" cries Mrs. Moberley at the top of her voice; pursuing her now departed handmaid with a hospitable scream.

"I hope not, for his sake, poor devil!" says Micky, with a noisy laugh; "you must excuse my laughing, but you people really have the worst small beer in Europe! where on earth do you get it from?"

Absorbed as Joan is in the joy of her posy, she cannot resist lifting her eyes to give him one glance of silent indignation; but Mrs. Moberley begins a weak and long-winded explanation of how it used to come from the Blue Posts; and though it is mostly sour now, yet that the old man is as honest an old man as you would see in a summer day, etc., etc.

Joan has turned away to the window to gloat over her treasures, ashamed that any one should see the joy painted on all her face.

"If it came from Covent Garden," says Di, joining her, "it could not have cost him a penny less than a guinea! Bobby Butler's that he gave Bell for the Fryars' New Year's Ball came to fifteen shillings! he told me so himself; and it was not half so big or so choice as this."

"A guinea! fifteen shillings?" cries Micky contemptuously; "you may depend upon it it did not cost him a penny! of course it came out of their own houses; the only wonder is that he did not think of so obvious an attention before."

"I wonder," says Bell, advancing with inquisitive haste to join her sister and cousin —"I wonder if there is not a note amongst them? in novels there always is a *billet doux* under the leaves—do look, Joan—nay" (giggling, as Joan turns away with reddened cheeks and an angry "pooh!") "now I am sure that there is, and that she is trying to find it without our seeing!"

"Examine it for yourself, then!" cries Joan tragically, holding out her nosegay, yielding it to Bell's ravaging desecrating hands; and looking on with an inward writhing as her cousin lifts each airy petal, parts each slender stem, to peep and dig and ferret between. In vain.

"I never can see the object of cramming bouquets full of this stuff!" says Micky in a hold-cheap voice; spitefully touching with his solid forefinger a fragile spray of maidenhair; "it dies before you can say 'knife' and shrivels up to an unsightly little black wisp!"

"I suppose that we have seen the last of them now," says Bell, with envious tone, reluctantly restoring her scented load. "I suppose, Joan, that you will take them up to your room now, and keep them there!"

"Put them into your jug," says Di kindly; "I should — and cut their stalks every day; your room will smell like a greenhouse!"

" Why should I be so greedy ?" says Joan, with reluctant magnanimity; " why should not we all have the benefit of them ?—that is " (retreating a little, and holding up her hand as a shield against Micky, who is advancing his blunt nose, with the evident intention of burying it among the orchids and gardenias), " that is—all we inmates of the house."

" I wish," says Bell, recovering her complexion and her interest in the subject—" I wish that some one would induce Sarah to be dressed a little earlier than usual to-day; he is pretty sure to look in, in the course of the afternoon, to be thanked !"

" If you want her to be spoken to, my dear," replies Mrs. Moberley in a whining tone, with her eyes aimlessly fixed on the blind, which is pulled up awry, and on which ancient rain stains make a yellow zig-zag; " you must do it yourself, for I tell you plainly I dare not ! it is as much as my place is worth, as they say ; she would make no more of giving me warning than I should of blowing my nose ! I am sure I do not know what the girls are coming to ! as Mrs. Green said the other day, there are no girls any-where !"

CHAPTER XIV.

HE next day is Sunday—a day to which Joan has been looking forward with some dread, as it is to witness her *début* at the Helmsley garrison church, which her cousins weekly frequent with pious regularity, winter and summer, come rain, come shine. For the first four Sundays of her stay with them she has succeeded in avoiding this ordeal: firstly, by a headache; secondly, by an ostentatiously displayed cold; thirdly, by a wet day, and the plea of easily spoiled crape; and fourthly, by feigned over fatigue from a long walk on the previous day. But this morning all these pretexts fail her. She has plainly no cold, nor would it be possible for any one with such clearly bright eyes and such delicately healthy cheeks to lay claim to a headache. It is not raining, and she took no walk yesterday ; to worship God with the soldiers must she therefore unavoidably go. Three miles there and three miles back, and for all that distance no more shade than you could cover with a penny-piece. A hot May sun brazenly staring, and a graceless wind catching up the dust in its spiteful hands and thrusting it down your reluctant throat and into your winking eyes. A day like a handsome shrew, goodly to look at, fresh and finely tinted, hateful to feel.

Mrs. Moberley, whose fondness for the military is hardly inferior to that of her daughters, has set off half an hour earlier to "take her time," as she says. By-and-by they overtake her, "larding," like Falstaff, "the lean earth," the wind faithfully outlining her bounteous form as she struggles against it, and her shawl forming a playful balloon at her back--" Faint yet pursuing."

As they pass a quiet little church with bells invitingly ringing, Joan makes a despairing stand, weary of the unending struggle with her heavy crape tail, which will decline from her arm into the dust, most weary of the sun, the blast, the audacious fat flies.

"Why should not we go in here?" she asks, looking longingly at the gray walls and the arched door.

"Nobody does," replies Bell, trenchantly quickening her pace; "none of them do. Sometimes they go to St. Chad's in the afternoon because the music is good, but never here" (nodding contemptuously at the despised place of worship). "One sees nothing but a few fusty tradespeople."

They have reached the haven at length, and are deposited in a pew, three in a row— Joan, more in accordance with their wishes than her own, between her two cousins—a

pew with a first-rate prospect. From it one
can see soldiers in profile, soldiers in rear,
soldiers in three-quarter. The Misses Moberley, having hurried through their pre-
liminary prayer and smoothed their refractory
locks and feathers, are now prepared for de-
votion and enjoyment; nor are they selfishly
anxious to keep either their pleasure or their
information to themselves. In whatever
ignorance of the domestic details of the
170th Joan has entered the church, they are
determined that she shall leave it in no such
case.

From the moment of their establishment
in the pew she is subject to an alternate
nudging and loud whispering into her reluctant ears. "Do you see that woman
coming up the chancel in the prune silk?
That is Mrs. Simpson; her husband is adju-
tant. She gave a garden-party the other
day, and asked everybody but us. It poured
rain; we were so glad." From the other
side: "That is Mrs. Allen in the fifth pew

on the left in the side aisle; she never returned our call. She gives herself great airs
because the General once sent his carriage
for her." This last piece of information is
conveyed in so raised a key that Joan looks
apprehensively round and cries, "Sh!"

The entrance of clergy and choir causes a
slight lull in the conversation. Everybody
stands up: in this position many new dis-
coveries as to who is in church and who is
not are made. The organ plays, the ex-
hortation is read. By-and-by they reach
the Litany. With face down sunk on her
slender black-clad hands, Joan is joining with
more heartfelt earnestness than ever in her
life before in the congregational cry of "Good
Lord, deliver us!" She has a vague feeling
that it is from Portland Villa, from Bell,
from squalor, from little sordid trials and
mean afflictions that she is begging to be
delivered. As she so pitifully and yearningly
prays, she lifts her face, and her sad look
wanders idly round the strange unfriendly

church, and over the many strange unfriendly
faces—they are so many, and not one friend
amongst them all.   Her eyes move indifferently, inattentively, from one to the other
in lack-lustre survey, when suddenly they
stop, and a little flash of clear bright joy
darts into their dolorous blue depths.

Is not that a friend who, so far away, so
almost out of sight, so nearly hidden by the
intervening red bodies of Micky Jackson and
half a dozen other light infantry, is leaning
his sunshiny head against a stone pillar in
abstract meditation or in sleep?   One can
see nothing of him but his back—a good
vigorous flat back—and the satiny sweep of
his straight brown locks.   Has he come to
Helmsley church to be thanked for his nosegay? for it is Wolferstan!   No sooner has
she recognised him than she stoops her head
again, and hides the cheeks that she feels
have grown suddenly warmly pink on her
open prayer-book, while above the drone of
the clergyman and the monotonous chorister

voices she hears the beating of her own loud heart.

"I am too glad!" she says to herself, shrinking frightened from the unused sensation of joy, "much too glad. Why should I be? there is no reason—none!"

Anon she steals another look. He has turned his profile towards her and his roving eye is wandering over the bent heads of the kneeling worshippers in evident search. There is no doubt that it is he : that broad gray eye, bold and mirthful, the clear window to such a goodly prosperous house, the *découpé* nostril, the *debonnair* lips, the shorn square chin.

"There is no doubt that I am dreadfully glad," she says to herself remorsefully, "and why, in Heaven's name, should I be?"

So she resolutely and ruthlessly keeps her eyes hidden and averted from that pleasant sight, nor takes one other glance. That is, not till the very end; not till—at the welcome signal of the benediction—all, both wakeful and sleepful, have sprung alertly to their feet. Then she lets her looks stray hastily once again to the distant pillar. Has he seen her? Probably not. His part of the church is drained by a distant door. He will probably depart without ever having been aware of her neighbourhood.

"So much the better," she says inwardly; but, even while so thinking, her fingers fidget uneasily with her prayer-book. Tall as she is, she raises herself furtively a little on her toes—her one chance of being discovered lies in her height and her black weeds.

"You need not be in a hurry, Joan," says Bell in a final whisper, noting her cousin's restlessness. "We always let them go out first—they pass by this pew—here they come, how their swords clatter!"

At length—at length—in the wake of many red tunics, they leave the church and reach the porch, only to find it filled with a discomfited crowd. For the face of the

day is changed; the brazen sun, the sickly
glare are gone—effaced by one giant rain-
cloud which has swept over the sky and is
angrily hurling its watery load to earth; the
wind, lowered, but not yet sunk, and still
spiteful as ever, is driving the heavy drops
into the faces and against the Sunday clothes
of the shrinking townsfolk in the porch.

Those who, prophetically wise, have
brought mackintoshes or waterproofs with
them are complacently enduing them. Those
who have not are enviously eying them.
Among the latter class is the Moberley
family. No protection whatever against the
weather have they, but flimsiest gaudiest
parasols; and on poor Diana's head flourishes
the beloved plume of paradise, which every
Sunday moves from her hat to her bonnet,
and every Monday moves back again from
her bonnet to her hat.

" It is good weather for young ducks, and
that is all that one can say !" says Mrs.
Moberley, with her usual slipshod happy-go-

lucky philosophy, gazing at the mad little muddy river which is racing down the church path.

Joan's eyes are directed, not towards the hostile weather, but towards the people still issuing from the church. Alas ! they have all come forth now; even the galleries and organ-loft are emptied and he is not amongst them. Her prognostic is fulfilled—he has departed without ever suspecting her near-ness. As she so thinks, with a private low sigh, her attention and her eyes are both recalled by a hasty breathless voice at her ear. It is Micky, who, with raindrops racing down his nose, with deeper red stains on his wet red tunic, panting yet triumphant, stands before her, with a large umbrella in his hand.

" Miss Dering—you have no umbrella !—I saw that you had not—I have been to fetch one for you—sexton's house—sexton's wife—hold it over you—no chance of its clearing—set off at once !"

" My aunt has no umbrella either," answers

Joan coldly, shrinking back farther into the
shelter of the porch.

" What does he care for that ?" says Mrs.
Moberley, with a good-humoured chuckle.
" Never mind, my dear. I am not sugar or
salt either."

" But Bell—Di—the alpacas !" cries Joan,
looking round with hasty wistfulness, and
greedily snatching at the nearest excuse.

" I am sorry that I cannot divide myself
and my umbrella by three !" says Micky
jocosely, having recovered his breath and his
coherence ; " but, as I cannot, I must repeat
my offer."

" Never mind us !" says Diana stoically,
winking away a very small tear, which had
been called into being by the callous indifference to her fate displayed by her old friend.
" He is quite right—you are of much more
consequence."

" Get along with you !" says Mrs. Moberley heartily, giving her a little friendly push,
never doubting that a compunctious delicacy

is the only motive for her niece's hanging
back; " we must take our chance; and as to
the alpacas, why, your crape would buy them
over and over again!"

Thus urged and encouraged by her relatives,
what remains for Joan to do but to step out
into the large resolute rain under the ægis of
the sexton's wife's roomy umbrella? She
does it as loathly as a cat would. Up the
swimming church path, through the church
gate, out into the swimming road. At least
the choking dust which rose to one's eyes is
changed to mud, which can assault one no
higher than one's ankles.

In wrathful—if ungratefully irrationally
wrathful—silence, Joan stalks along, and
though his legs are longer than hers, he has
some ado to keep up with her without de-
generating into a run. At last :

"Do not you think," says Micky in
mild remonstrance (for, in a *tête-à-tête*, the
swagger which the knowledge of the in-
variable Moberley support and applause

alone maintains wholly disappears) — " do
not you think that if you walk so very fast
you will be out of breath before you reach
Portland Villa ?"

" Thank you, no."

" Do you call it quite three miles to
Helmsley ?" pursues Mr. Brand, trying to
be conversationally agreeable on indifferent
subjects. " I should think that it could not
be more than two and three-quarters."

" Quite three—more than three !" replies
Joan, with a despondent glance at the long
stretch of wet straight road before her.

" I think" (diffidently) " that if you would
allow me to come a little nearer to you I
could protect you better ; the points of the
umbrella are dripping on to your shoulder."

" Thank you !" (very hastily). " It is of
no consequence."

" You " (with a good deal of hesitation)—
" you would not like to take my arm, I suppose ?"

" Thank you, no !"

A silence. Still mightily striding through the storm.

"I wonder what has become of the others?" begins Micky again presently, with an air of complacency. "I hope they are not getting a drenching."

"I do not see how they can well help it," replies Joan dryly; "and Diana had a cold already."

"Poor girl!" (in a tone of ostentatious indifference); "how very unlucky!"

Through the bleak suburbs between the scaffolding poles and the forlorn brick heaps they are passing, when another noise mixes with that of the rain and the wind in their ears. A noise of wheels coming up behind them. Some happy person who has a carriage, and presumably has not a Micky, bowling safely and dryly home from church. As the wheels come up with them their noise ceases. The happy person is apparently stopping beside them. In quick wonder, just flavoured with an unlikely hope, Joan looks round, in time to see Wolferstan throwing the reins to his groom, and jumping down out of his phaeton into the mud : on his figure is a wet great-coat, and on his face a rather displeased expression of pleasure.

"Miss Dering, will you allow me to take you home ? at least, you will be able to keep yourself drier—may I help you in at once ?— that is, of course, unless" (with a slight and sulky glance at Micky) "you prefer walking."

"Is it likely ?" she answers, with a smile all sunshine—not mixed sunshine and rain like his ; "am I quite a fish, to be so fond of the water ?" and so gives him her hand ; and setting her light foot on the step springs gaily in, leaving Micky, unthanked, alone, with his giant umbrella, in the mire.

How one's point of view changes ! Five minutes ago Joan was ready to maintain that there were nearer four than three miles between Helmsley and Portland Villa ; now she is prepared to swear that there are not more than two, and of those two, one, through her ill-advised hasty striding, is already over-past.

"You never walked with me under an umbrella!" is Wolferstan's first reproachful observation, as through the storm they merrily fly.

"It was always fine weather when I was with you," replies Joan; nor, until she has uttered it, does she see the double meaning of the answer.

"Under an umbrella," repeats Wolferstan, frowning a little; the idea evidently rankling in his mind; "there is such intimacy in an umbrella."

"Yes, there is," answers Joan, shuddering a little at the recollection of Micky's eyes amorously glowering at her from beneath the great cotton mushroom.

"What a pace you must have walked at!" continues the young man, still chafing; "whose fault was that—yours or his?"

"Mine."

" You must have run."

" I did nearly."

" I should have overtaken you long ago," says Anthony, with an air of irritation ; " only that I was fool enough to wait at the church—I forgot all about that other door."

" You saw me in church, then ?"

" Yes, but not till the sermon" (in an aggrieved voice).

" Ah ! I saw you in the Litany" (with a soft tone of superiority).

How quickly the horse is trotting. At this rate in five minutes they will be at Portland gate. How smartly they pass through the slackening rain, while the boisterous wind sings with uncouth jollity in their ears.

" What a long time it seems since I was here last," says Wolferstan presently, looking affectionately at the wet May garlands in the hedges—at the roadside trees—at the flat green fields.

"Exactly a month—four weeks yesterday," answers Joan. Then, seeing on his face more complacency at the accuracy of her memory than she thinks either wholesome or desirable, she hastens to add : "I have a wonderful memory for small incidents : it is a month since you were here; three weeks since the piano-tuner; ten days since the sweeps."

The complacency disappears, as she had meant it. The greatest coxcomb cannot be too much exalted by being bracketed with a piano-tuner and sweeps.

"Four weeks, instead of the one that I meant," he says reflectively. "Do you know why it has been four weeks instead of one ?"

"Yes," she answers sedately, "I know."

"Why ?"

"Because you were better amused where you were."

He shakes his head.

"Wrong. Not but what I was very much amused too," he adds conscientiously; "for the matter of that I mostly am. For my part"—with a light laugh—" I should like to live for ever; the longer my innings are the better I shall be pleased; but that was not the reason."

She is silent.

"Why do not you ask me what it was," he asks in a sort of pet, "when you see that I am longing to be questioned? You might have the civility to oblige me."

"Suppose that I do not care to hear?" she says, with a small fine smile.

"Then you ought to care," he answers gaily. "Whether you care or not you must hear. Are you listening?"

"Yes."

"You know," he goes on, becoming grave and speaking seriously, "I am sure I told you, that I have no great belief in myself. I have never had much reason for any; and you disbelieved in me so thoroughly too that I thought perhaps, after all, you might be right."

"Yes."

"Do you know," he continues, reddening slightly and speaking quickly, "I wish you would not make me tell you these sort of humiliating things, but you do. Do you know that more than once I have been ready to cut my throat about a woman on Monday, and by Saturday have forgotten what shape her nose was?"

"I quite believe it," very dryly.

"I thought—no, I did not think—I had a faint hope that. this—this attack might be something of the same kind; at least, thought I, I would give myself the chance—"

"Yes."

"Well, at the end of the first week—"

"At the end of the first week," she says, speaking with a red smile and a pretty curly lip—"at the end of the first week my nose was growing an indistinct memory; at the end of the second week you were not quite sure that I had a nose; at the end of the third week—"

"At the end of the third week," interrupts Anthony, taking the words out of her mouth and looking down on her boldly and fondly with his happy gray eyes, " I began to blame all eyes that were not blue ; and yet it would be monotonous if they were all blue, would not it? At the end of the fourth week I got into the train, *voila tout.*"

" *Voila tout,* indeed !" says Joan, with half a laugh and half a sigh, " for here we are."

It is true. They have reached the gate, through the bars of which six black *retroussé* faces are gravely regarding them. The rain has ceased, the great sun is blithely shouldering aside the sulky clouds, the gutters run less madly down the road, the stooped flowers and the lashed grasses begin to think of raising themselves again.

"See how fine it is," says Wolferstan, directing her attention to the young laugh which is beginning to break gently out over earth's face. " Why may not we lengthen a little our drive ?"

" On the other hand, why should we ?" she answers.

There is that in her voice which makes him feel that further pressing would be useless; her tone is so low that it is almost drowned by the voices of the dogs, who by this time have issued from the gate, and thankful for anything which is likely to disperse the *ennui* attendant on Sunday, are giving a hideous outdoor concert round the ill-starred vehicle. Two are jumping teasingly up at the horse's nose ; three are making playful snaps at his heels; while Mr. Brown, standing on his hind legs—in which biped attitude he looks like a very plain man—with one forepaw on the axle of the wheel, is peering upwards with his near-sighted eyes to see who the inmates of the carriage are. In silence Wolferstan lifts his young companion down to earth. She had meant to jump from the high wheel, but he has baffled her by taking her in his arms. He is following her now into the house. Becoming aware of his intention, she turns and faces him.

" You are coming in ?" she says doubtfully, standing in the gateway as if to hinder his entrance.

" I think so," he answers modestly ; " am I not?"

For an instant she stands irresolute : the bluff wind making her heavy gown and her lithe body sway a little, like a tall pale flower, and the blood sending crimson messages up into her cheeks. Then she speaks :

" If you like, and on one condition."

" What condition ?" (laughing) ; " that it is the last offence of the kind ?"

" No, not that."

" What then ?"

" You may come," she says, turning her very-much-in-earnest eyes and her face swept by a great carnation flush to his; " on condition that you promise not to stay to luncheon."

He looks surprised.

" I promise."

" However much they may press you ?"

" Yes."

" Not pie-crust promise — mind — a real solemn binding oath ?"

" A real solemn binding oath !"

She draws a long breath of relief.

" Then you may come and welcome !"

He laughs dryly.

" You are very hospitable !"

" It is the truest hospitality !" she answers.

CHAPTER XV.

CCOMPANIED by a vanguard, rear-guard, and body-guard of little dogs, all fantastically dancing round and squeaking with ecstasy over their recovered Joan (for though they sometimes show their affection injudiciously, yet, indeed, they love her very dearly), Wolferstan makes his first entry into Portland Villa. Miss Dering could have wished that the smell of roast mutton had been less mightily and universally pervasive. The whole house appears to have turned, in honour of Wolferstan, into hot mutton fat. She steals a covert look at him to see how he is bearing it. Manners forbid him to

hold his nose, and so good an actor is he that
he seems to be inhaling the warm tallow with
no apparent inconvenience or di··relish.

The drawing-room is undoubtedly un-
changed since before she went to church, but
yet it seems to her a far tawdrier little desert
than it did then; the woolly antimacassar
more faded, the spar and Bohemian glass
more flimsily gim-crack, the dust on the carpet
a fathom deeper. She sits dejectedly down
on the music-stool. After all, though the
music-stool gives one some frights, it is really
more dependable than most of the other
chairs. He stands on the hearth-rug racking
his brains for something complimentary, and
at the same time not too flagrantly untruthful
to say about the apartment. As his look
wanders round in the vain search for something to commend, it falls on his own flowers,
standing in a gaudy jug, and already beginning to yellow and shrivel in this atmosphere
of gas and mutton.

"Why do you keep them here?" he asks

in a discontented voice; "to be a house of entertainment for every nose in the family. I meant them for *you*."

" Would you like me to keep them in my boudoir ?" she asks, with gentle irony. " Do not you know that poor people must have their luxuries in common ? In poverty there can be no privacy."

He looks dissatisfied.

" This is your only sitting-room, then ?" in a voice out of which he tries to keep the disgusted surprise.

" The only one."

" You all sit in it always ?"

" Yes."

" Mrs. Moberley, the two Misses Moberley, and you ?"

" Yes."

" If I came I should find you *all* here ?"

" Yes."

A little pause, Wolferstan's eyes uncomfortably taking in the full meanness, threadbareness, vulgarity of the little room. Then he speaks in a low and almost awe-struck key:

"Every day and all day for the last month, and every day and all day for the next month, and the month after that, and the month after that again—"

"Not all day," she interrupts gently; "sometimes — often — I sit in my bed-room."

"By way of an improvement?" in quick and ironical interrogation.

"I am rubbing up my old learning, such as it is," she answers, smiling a little, "and one must be alone to do that."

Another little silence.

"Is this to go on for ever?" breaks out the young man suddenly, breathing short and quick as if oppressed by some weight (perhaps it is the tallow that is beginning at last to tell upon him).

"Nothing goes on for ever," she answers gravely. "It is this thought that I think would keep me from being ever too glad, and that now saves me from being too dismal."

He has thrown himself on the little sofa, and, with head down bent and hands thrust disconsolately through his hair, is staring blankly at the carpet. He looks so thoroughly miserable that Mr. Brown, who has a kind heart, goes up and begins to lick the end of his nose to comfort him.

" Sometimes," continues Joan in her soft sad voice, while her eyes wander idly out through the window to the grass-plot, and the hedge ablaze in new green in the stormy sunshine, " sometimes I wish that I had come here long ago, when I was a child. Sometimes one seems old at twenty; to change all one's likes and dislikes; all one's points of view and habits of thought; but then, again," shaking her head slowly, " I think that—no, it is best as it is; I have those years always to the good; they are my honey that I live upon now in this my winter."

He has lifted his head, and as she so
soberly and sweetly speaks, an idiotic and
unheard-of longing comes over him to snatch
her just as she is, sitting poised on her
rickety music-stool in all her forlorn black
—to snatch, I say, Mrs. Moberley's niece
to his heart, and, piling upon her a hundred unseemly fond names, ask her to let
him try to make life summer again to
her. In order to save himself from yielding to so absurd an impulse, he gets up
hastily and walks to the window. Through
his heart is blowing as stormy a wind
as that which outside is fiercely showing the underside of all the leaves, and
making the tree-tops bow and creak. By-
and-by he turns towards her, and speaks
abruptly :

"Which is your chair? which do you
usually sit in ?"

"That one," she answers, pointing.

He mistakes the direction of her finger,
and is about to sit down on an apparently

whole and healthy chair, when the girl's warning cry stops him.

" Not that one, not that one !   It is not safe, it has only three legs."

" Then why, in Heaven's name, do they keep it ?" asks Anthony in genuine astonishment, eying the decrepit piece of furniture which has so nearly wrought his woe.

" There are so few without it," replies Joan humbly, looking ruefully round on the poor and scanty household stuff.

Whether his experience of the one chair has inspired him with a rooted distrust of them all, or whether he fears a recurrence of his former undesirable impulse is unknown, but he walks again to the window and watches the Campidoglio cat, who, having made herself into an arch, and stiffened her tail to the likeness of a poker, is boxing the angry dog's ears.   In a moment, however, he utters an exclamation of astonishment.

" Is it possible ?" he cries, turning to her with a vexed expression.   " They are back already—how quickly they must have walked. They must have *run !*"

He says it in all innocence, not in any way connecting their speed with himself; but one glance at Joan's confused face, shame-reddened cheeks, and drooped eyes lets light in upon him. It is to make *his* acquaintance that the dauntless Moberleys have raced through the mire.

In two minutes they are all in the room —all three—yes, even Mrs. Moberley. If she had taken such violent exercise every day for the last ten years, she would not now be the sized Mrs. Moberley that she is.

"How do you do, Colonel Wolferstan?" she cries, advancing with right-hand far out-stretched, and as much warmth of greeting as if he were a long-lost prodigal son. "Very glad to see you in my house; though it is the first time, I hope it will not be the last by many ! You do not know my girls, I think ? No ? Never happened to meet ? My eldest,"

proudly producing Bell; " my youngest !"
affably indicating Di.

" We have often felt as if we knew you !"
says Bell in a languishing tone, hazarding a
glance of sugared bashfulness, " meeting you
so often in society."

" Speak for yourself, Bell !" says Diana
gruffly ; " I never thought that I knew
Colonel Wolferstan—I always knew that I
did not."

" I hope you will always know me for the
future," says Anthony, rather embarrassed
between an intense inclination to laugh and
as intense a compassion for Joan. " For-
tunately down here I have not a double as I
have in London, where, in consequence, I am
mostly cut by the people I know, and greeted
by the people I do not know."

" How awkward !" sighs Bell. Her head
is still on one side, and her voice like that
with which the wedded turtle-dove in the
wood apostrophises her mate.

" Micky was in a fine *fanteague* when we

met him," says Mrs. Moberley in a loud and perfectly audible aside to Joan, " at being left in the lurch. Do not think that I blame you, child," noting the crimson distress of her niece's face, and mistaking the cause ; " do not think that I blame you! Who would not keep a dry skin if they could ? For my part," turning again to Wolferstan, " I cannot think how you could tear yourself away from Town just at this gay time ; I can assure you that you will find us all as dull as ditch-water."

" We have not been up at all this year," says Bell affectedly, as if a season were with her an annual occurrence.

" We never do !" cries Diana, flushing. " Do you know," lifting a large pair of shy eyes to their guest's face—" do you know that I have never been in London in my life ?"

" This year, at least, you have no loss," he answers civilly. " The heat has been something unheard of—ninety in the shade the day I came down."

" You do not say so !" says Mrs. Moberley

in a high staccato key of astonishment. "We have been regretting that we had put up our furs. We should have had them out again only that it seemed a pity to take them out of the camphor." A moment later: "You will stay to din—luncheon, I mean—of course. I must tell Sarah to lay another place; you will hardly believe it, but she would never do it out of her own head."

She is on her way to the door when, mindful of his oath, he arrests her progress.

"Thank you very much—nothing I should like better! but I am afraid it is impossible. I—I—have an engagement at home."

"Now what engagement can you have on a Sunday?" asks Mrs. Moberley, with affectionate incredulity. "I will not take 'No!' We can offer you only a plain roast leg of mutton"—this information at least is needless—"but I daresay you do not dislike a plain joint for a change!"

"I love it!" he answers, laughing, thankful for even this flimsy excuse to indulge his mirth, which otherwise he feels that he would be constrained to indulge without a pretext. One more glance at the fat pathos of Bell's lackadaisical peony face will, he is aware, be the death of him. But, in mid-mirth, he suddenly stops: he has caught one look of Joan's face—her face of abject entreaty and agonised appeal, and his laughter dies.

Rebutting with civil persistence the importunities of Mrs. Moberley and of her eldest daughter, he is at length allowed to depart.

"Well, we do really know him at last!" cries Bell, with a long-drawn breath of triumph, before he is well out of the room; " what a mercy the rain was!"

" He was laughing so that he could hardly speak," says Diana in a mortified tone. " I watched him down the drive—he was shaking all over!"

As for Joan, she has rushed up to her room, and, flinging herself on the bed, has buried her miserable burning face on the little hard pillow.

" It will kill me !" she says, with strangled sobs — strangled for fear of being heard through the thin floor. " It will kill me ! as long as they did not know him it was bearable—henceforth it will be unbearable !"

END OF VOL. I.

BILLING AND SONS, PRINTERS, GUILDFORD, SURREY.

www.ingramcontent.com/pod-product-compliance
Lightning Source LLC
Chambersburg PA
CBHW020322140726
47905CB00013B/2269